Low Road to Heaven

*(A woman he tried to know,
a son he had never known,
a God he thought he knew)*

Rod Loché

PublishAmerica
Baltimore

W9-BIE-654

ISBN: 1-4241-5009-4
PUBLISHED BY PUBLISHAMERICA, LLLP
www.publishamerica.com
Baltimore

Printed in the United States of America

Dedicated to South Bay Community Church
This book is as much your accomplishment as it is mine.

Acknowledgments

My sincere thanks to...

My editor, Mrs. Diana Schaufler, your input and reassurance was invaluable.

April Lomas, John Bautista, Marcie Harding, and Gwen Senegal: It was your encouragement that allowed this dream to become a reality.

Karen Defrantz for freely lending your talents.

My friends and family at South Bay Community Church for your prayers and continued support.

Dr. Stanley B. Long: I thank God for the gift of your teaching and your inspiration.

My parents, Henry and Evelyn Loche: You have always been there in every way possible. What more could a son ask for?

Darren, Lionel, and Mary: Siblings don't come any better.

And finally, to my wife Patty and my daughters Crystal, Jasmine, and Jahlan: the ways you have blessed my life are more numerous than the stars. Thank you for everything.

Chapter 1

There is always a danger that we will permit the means by which we live to replace the ends for which we live, the internal to become lost in the external.
Martin Luther King

Joseph sat stiff. His stomach was tight and his knee couldn't seem to stop bouncing. He had been told by more than a couple of people that this final stage of his interview was a mere formality. But even so, he couldn't seem to relax and portray the confident image he had shown to himself in the mirror so many times the days before. The table in front of him stretched on and on to no end it seemed. All of these suited gentlemen sitting before him he knew personally. He had enjoyed a dinner at each and every home on numerous occasions. They had studied together, played ball together, he had even gone on vacation with a couple of these men. But today was a different day. Somehow, none of that mattered. There were no jokes and no smiling faces. Just the eyes of concern focused on him, surely wondering: What has this young man to offer that would move me to follow him? He kept his hands clenched tightly because he knew the shaking hands would be all too noticeable were he to relax. The room seemed to be shrinking smaller and smaller. He had to get out, just so he could clear his head of the doubt closing in around him.

"Can I—"

But before he could finish the question, the double doors to the side of the room swung open.

In walked Louis Wendell. He strolled in casually, as though he didn't realize that he was late. He was dressed in a blue pinstriped suit. It was single-breasted, even though he was well known for his many appealing double-breasted ones. He took his usual seat at the head of the table opposite Joseph. Before he spoke, he took in a huge sigh as if to say, "I'd rather be at home with my wife, but I guess we can go ahead and get this over with anyway." Then, in a somber baritone voice, Pastor Wendell broke the silence.

"Well, Mr. Shaw, it appears we've come to the final stage of our interview process. I think I can speak for all of us when I say we are extremely pleased with everything we've seen and heard up to this point. Now, regardless of what you've probably heard about this final stage in the process, it really isn't as bad as most assume. This is really just the point in the interview where we try to find out exactly what it was that brought you here to us—right here, right now. Both I, and the Deacon Board, feel that the associate pastor at a church as prominent as De Angeles Memorial needs to be more than a student of the Word. He needs to be more than a pillar of the community. He needs to be more than what is written down in the position description found in the church bylaws. That type of man is an honorable one indeed, and we value that man in our church. But what we want to verify is that the man we put in the position of associate pastor is a man whose life is guided by the hand of the Almighty."

Pastor Wendell's eyes stayed focused on Joseph as he spoke. He hoped to get some idea of just how well the young man was staying in tune with what was being said.

"You see, people today go to church and profess the name of the Lord to the highest mountaintop. They keep the Word of God on their lips in conversation. They believe that they're sincere in their praise, and I'm not saying they aren't. What I am saying is that they don't always have that trust in God that puts one's mind at ease when the storm is on its way. The thing that lets them take comfort in the midst of burning flames. That kind of peace is a valuable thing. When people encounter someone who has that peace inside of 'em, they gravitate to it. It pierces the soul and finds its home in the heart of anyone it touches. Yeah, it's worth more than gold."

Mr. Wendell continually and strategically took long pauses between each statement. With each pause, the words seemed to gain more and more weight as they penetrated Joseph's consciousness. But no matter how long the pause, not a soul dared attempt to jump in.

After closing his eyes to ponder the seriousness of the moment, Pastor Wendell continued. "Now, finding out *who* has it is something else altogether. Do you simply ask somebody, 'Do you have peace with the Lord?' Do you have someone fill out a questionnaire? What if we don't all agree on who possesses this spirit-given gift to lead and who doesn't? Then what do we do? Well, after immense discussion among everybody involved in the decision-making process, we decided that the best way to tell what's truly in a man's soul is to listen. Listen to him talk about himself and his relationship with God. Why does he even pursue a relationship with God? How did his life come to that place where he knows that there is nothing else worth living for, nothing else worth loving for, or dying for? You see, the spiritual journey one experiences throughout life is what shapes a man's inner self, and that inner self is what bonds us with the Almighty. Now, the tradition of personal *testimony* in the Christian church goes back quite a ways."

The word struck Joseph like a hurled stone to the back of the head. His mind began to jump between concern and panic.

Testimony! What testimony? What am I gonna say? Oh no, I can't believe this.

He tried not to show the distress on his face, and he certainly didn't want to miss anything important being said, but it was hard to try to balance fear and attentiveness as he kept his eyes focused on the pastor.

"Formally, the personal testimony, or *Confession*, if you will, takes on four different stages: "Stage one, the life prior to finding God.

Stage two, the events in that life that led up to the spiritual awakening."

As hard as he struggled to remain composed, Joseph couldn't keep the anxiety from creeping into his head. *They all know the ugly details of my life. I can't go through any of that again. They just want to hear all about what a terrible son I was. Whenever I start to think that it's behind me, it comes back.* He again told himself to stay calm and concentrate, but the war raged on.

The pastor continued, "Stage three, the actual event, or encounter with God. And stage four, the blessed life that results from being one with the Lord. Now we understand that every man's life is different. You need not follow everything I'm telling you to the letter. You can start where you feel it is appropriate to start and finish the same way. But one thing I want to caution you against is leaving things out, or glossing over something because you feel we already know about it. Maybe some of us do and maybe some of us don't, but what we are interested in is how *you* see it—how you feel about whatever happened or didn't happen."

As he spoke, each man in the room remained completely intent on what was being said. Nobody took their eyes off the pastor, except to take a quick glance in Joseph's direction to see how the young man was taking it all in.

"You and your family have been with De Angeles Memorial from the start. Shoot, your grandfather *was* the start. Most of us here know a lot about the road you took to get here, but I don't want you to talk to us like you're filling in the gaps. This isn't about us trying to find out all the details of your personal life. It's about us trying to find out the details of what brought you to Jesus. Now don't worry about talking for too long or too short a period of time. If you feel you can say what you need to say in ten minutes, then that's fine with us. On the other hand, if you need two hours, that's fine too. Now before you begin, uh, does anybody have anything they feel they may need to add for Mr. Shaw?"

James Quincy was Joseph's closest friend on the Deacon Board, and as one of Joseph's main advocates for the associate pastor position, he was certain that his young friend was the right man for the job. James chimed in with a refreshing voice when he sensed that their applicant was turning to stone. "How about if we let him take five or ten minutes to get his thoughts in order before he gets started?"

Pastor Wendell gave a half smile, acknowledging that he had put the youngster in something of a tailspin. "Sure, he can take all the time he needs, but first, do you have any questions, Mr. Shaw?"

A quick, "No, sir," was all the reply Joseph could manage.

As he stood in the bathroom splashing cold water on his face, Joseph's thoughts were swirling around the room. *I can't believe they want me to do this. Grandpa Al had to know about this. Why didn't he tell me? I've never talked to anybody about what really brought me here.*

He remembered his grandfather's advice on the phone only hours ago: "Don't be afraid of what anybody may think. Say what comes from the heart, and be content with that."

They were the first thoughts of comfort to show up, and he really needed them.

I can do this. It's just talking, or telling a story.

But he was only half believing what he was telling himself as he stared into the mirror. Then he said a prayer. He was too conscious of the amount of time passing by to put much effort into it. He certainly didn't want to keep the Pastor Wendell waiting, but he was confident he was heard just the same.

What young Joseph Shaw did on that Saturday morning was exactly what his grandfather told him to do, and what his father would have wanted. Although it was unrehearsed, or perhaps *because* it was unrehearsed, Joseph spoke not just passionately about his past life, but honestly and movingly as well. He began about twelve years back when he was leaving to attend college in the South.

* * * * *

"Come on, Dad, you got to work with me here. You know I need some transportation when I'm out there."

The nineteen-year-old was loading his bags into the car, still clearly upset at not being able to take the 1987 Honda Prelude with him to school. Not quite six feet tall, and not nearly as filled out as he would have liked to be, Joseph was still a fairly nice-looking young man. With his hair closely clipped and his mustache trimmed daily, Joseph maintained a neat appearance that was somewhat contrary to the baggy jeans and often strange hairstyles that served as the trademark for his generation.

"So if I'm carrying a 3.0 after two semesters I get to take the car, right?"

"Yeah, I'll think about it."

Allen Henry Shaw, Jr. was not known to be an easily-swayed man. He was not tall, and not fat, but he was a big man. He was a very serious father in the opinion of literally everybody who knew him. He was not one to leave things to chance. Education and God were his priorities, and as far as he was concerned, *his* priorities were his son's priorities. He always appreciated Joseph's clean-cut appearance, but he often worried that his son didn't apply himself at school or to anything else as he should.

Joseph continued to press about the car, and also the credit card, but to no avail. He might have had more success had his older sister, Jasmine, been a co-signer for his cause, but as usual, she chose to side with her dad, leaving her baby brother to his own desperate demise.

"I don't know what you're complaining about. You're getting a free car in a year, and all you have to do is keep your grades up. Stop whining!"

Jasmine was undoubtedly her father's child, never one to make a decision that had not been well thought through. She was the clearest picture of control to all who knew her. Married just a little over a year now, she was expecting her first child. The new arrival—either Eric Joseph or Erica Josephine Woodfork (after the paternal grandmom or granddad)—would be her father's first grandchild. Her husband, Mark Woodfork, had been her high school sweetheart, and to those closest to them the marriage was both inevitable and welcomed.

Joseph chose to ignore his sister's addition to the argument, especially since she had no decision-making power.

"Well, what if I get like a 3.5 G.P.A. my first semester? You'll know I'm hittin the books if I get a 3.5, then can I get the car?"

To that, Dad turned toward his son, stared him directly pupil-to-pupil, and gave one of his signature responses to a desperate child. "Boy, you got too many wants and you don't know your needs—that's your problem."

The ride to the airport took the form of a lecture more than a conversation. Dad gave his son all the advice he could fit into a hundred mile trip.

"Make sure you fill out the grant application as soon as you have a free second. Don't bother with those fraternities, at least not during your freshman year. Maybe later on down the road you might have time for that stuff, but first you've got to get your grades on track and get acclimated to the campus. Try and do most of your hanging out on campus, there's no need to spend more time than is necessary hanging out around the city. You don't know anybody out there."

Joseph was upset, but as the drive went on his frustration gave way to a mounting excitement mixed with a touch of shaky nerves. As he stared out the window he silently bid goodbye to the city of De Angeles, the only town he had ever lived in.

He was thankful for the little city. To him, De Angeles had been the perfect place to create a treasure of boyhood memories. Lying on the outskirts of Sacramento, California, De Angeles was more a town than it was a city. People from other parts of the country always confused it with the more densely populated Los Angeles, but Joseph knew there was no comparison. De Angeles offered an ideal mixture of rural and suburban surroundings. The city itself was clearly rustic, but Sacramento, a stone's throw away, offered all the city appeal a young restless heart could hope for. And Joseph had made the best of both worlds.

He and Jasmine, although they never admitted it, had always enjoyed the walks home from school. Sometimes they walked with friends, and sometimes it was only the two of them. They both looked forward to sharing the day's events with one another during the forty-five minute trek, which in itself was odd in the beginning. During earlier years the siblings never seemed quite comfortable with sincere conversation. Joseph always suspected it was because he received more attention than his sister did.

He was an attractive child. People frequently commented on the likeness between he and his mom. This, Joseph relished, because Josephine Shaw was beautiful. Her skin was the shade of polished bronze and her greenish-colored eyes were shaped like almonds. Everyone said that his features were just the same. Even today, whenever he was complimented on his eyes, a picture of his mom's captivating face automatically popped into his head. When he would walk down the street with his hand in hers, people watched. He purposely appeared to ignore the envious eyes, but inside he gloated.

When Joseph was born, most expected that he would be named "Allen III." It wasn't until the last minute that his dad decided on the name "Joseph," after his mom. Some years ago after his mom's passing, Joseph overheard his dad say to someone that "When I first held him in my arms there was no denying that he was his mother's child. I had no choice but to name him Joseph."

He never really felt guilty for the attention he received because Jasmine seemed to be the jewel of her dad's eye. She had his wide smile and long legs. Even more noticeable than those was her unyielding will. Jasmine was strong in spirit, and as he got older Joseph began to realize that his sister's disposition would be more of a blessing than a burden.

There were countless days at school when being the younger brother of Jasmine Shaw turned out to be a fortunate reality, such as when her pretty friends doted over him in the presence of Charlene Keilough just so he could get her attention. Although Charlene never took the bait, looking back, the plan wasn't entirely fruitless. The doting itself was gratifying enough to have been well worth the effort.

As he rode in the car, he reminisced on past experiences that one way or another bound him to this city and this family. He wondered when he would see his school acquaintances again. He wondered if De Angeles would look the same when he returned. Then, suddenly, the deep voice of his dad that had been droning on continuously, summoned his undivided attention.

"Boy, are you listening to me? You don't need to get out there and start wasting time, you hear? You got to be handling business."

Joseph periodically glanced at his dad, and nodded in agreement, as the law was being laid down. But inside the young man's mind there was a bittersweet, nostalgic journey. He was moving on to the next stage in the life of Joseph Shaw, and he needed desperately to hold onto a couple of things that were near and dear to his practices of thought. Most of his friends were eager to leave their youthful adventures and experiences behind, but Joseph planned to make sure that certain memories would always be a part of him.

Chapter 2

The caged bird sings with a fearful trill
Of things unknown but longed for still
And his tune is heard on the distant hill
For the caged bird sings for freedom
Maya Angelou

As far back as Sharonda could remember her birthday had been her favorite day of the year. Christmas was really nice and offered a lot of days off from school too, but Christmas she had to share with everybody else. June 26th was hers and hers alone. The ice cream and cake were a particular highlight. There had always been many delicacies that she enjoyed much more than cake and ice cream, but none were accompanied by candles and singing. Nothing in the world commanded such respect upon its arrival at a kitchen table as a birthday cake. And with "HAPPY BIRTHDAY SHARONDA" scrawled across the top in more shades of pink, purple, and red than she would have otherwise known existed. The other 364 days of the year could never hope to measure up. It wasn't until years later that she would realize that not even a birthday cake in all its glory could sufficiently claim center stage in lieu of the loving affection of her parents.

On June 26th, Mitchell Atkins was always home taking

exceptional interest in his darling sweetheart. On June 26th there were no angry voices or sobbing cries heard between thin apartment walls, only loud music and boisterous talk of guests glad to be sharing in her special day. On June 26th the sky was always blue and the laughter would seem to last a little longer. Whether wearing her long purple dress that tied in the front or her pink flowered blouse with matching flowered jeans, she was always the belle of the ball, and every tight hug and soft kiss on the cheek reinforced this truth. Although she would never mention it to any of them, she knew that even her cake was always a bit sweeter than the cakes at the parties of her many friends and cousins.

At age four, after being instructed earlier on how to find her date of birth on the calendar, Sharonda came up with the idea for a household utopia. The plan was so simple she couldn't imagine why she hadn't come up with it before. With only a few hours of work, she had successfully, if not neatly, changed every day of the year to the 26th—well, almost every day. She had sense enough not to tamper with the two days that were designated mommy's birthday and daddy's birthday, but the rest she knew were expendable. Sharonda was shocked to find that her idea didn't go over too well with her parents. Why anybody should have taken issue with her adjustments was bewildering. In the end, it turned out that not even Sharonda herself knew of the falsities in her parents' assumption that gifts were the driving force behind the four-year-old's efforts.

Years later, Sharonda found herself still partial to cake and candles even though her parties had ceased long ago. The lasting effects of 364 days a year of fear, pain, and disappointment had blossomed into the stone will and resentment of a young woman, at best, uninterested in the world around her. Masked by a sweet smile, most were caught off-guard by her cold indifference soon after becoming acquainted with her.

Sharonda was attractive without trying to be, but that didn't stop her from taking exceptional pride in her appearance. In high school she had been very thin, but not long after graduation her shape began to show the curves she had always secretly desired. She always remembered hearing her dad joke about the voluptuous Pam Grier, and since then she knew that real women had curves. It never dawned on her that other men may have a totally different opinion on the matter. As an adult, her hair stayed perfect, and her clothes were up-to-date. Her tall frame and full lips caught the eye of most men who crossed her path, and she got immense joy from turning down the advances of one admirer after another. Her mom was not nearly as pretty, and Sharonda often wondered as a child if her parents' relationship would have been different had her mom been a more attractive woman. Just yesterday her mom had called with a nearly-two-weeks-late happy birthday message from her father. To Sharonda, the message was not worth the breath used to deliver it. Her mom was disappointed in her response.

"He should have said happy birthday for next year. At least he'd be early instead of being late."

"Why do you always have to be so negative? Can't you just say something nice for once?"

"I'll say something nice when he does something to deserve it! Calling to say happy birthday in July when my birthday is in June don't cut it!"

"I wish you would cut him a little slack. You know he loves you to death. He just ain't the most organized man in the world, that's all. He means well."

Now at age twenty-three, Sharonda could make her own cakes, pay her own bills, and when push came to shove, she had even managed to change her own motor oil once or twice. She was stronger than her mom; they both knew it. She often felt pity for her mother. Sharonda could never understand why June Atkins always managed to give more of herself than she could spare and get nearly nothing in return. She despised the men who took advantage of her mom's excessive devotion.

June Atkins was a beaten woman. There was a time in her life when she had been strong. She was student body president in junior high school. She even led the charge to get school dances brought back to Roosevelt Junior High when principal Cutley tried to cancel them because of lewd dancing. June Tyson (as she was then known) sent around a petition and even managed to get a number of parents involved. Before long, Mr. Cutley realized that little Miss Tyson was a force to be reckoned with. Two weeks later, there they all were, close to two-hundred greased-up and decked-out kids, swaying back and forth across the gymnasium floor to Smokey Robinson and the Miracles.

She can't quite put her finger on when it happened but at some point everything changed. She had no idea what happened to the little girl who stood nose-to-stomach with Principal Cutley and held her ground. Maybe it was the disappointment of realizing that a little girl from the wrong side of the tracks could not afford to go to college. Maybe it was the constant reflection of a teenage girl being only good for one thing seen in the eyes of boy after boy, then man after man.

Many nights she lay in her bed reliving her junior high school glory—how Smokey's voice sounded so smooth and sultry that night. She glanced through sleepy eyes at her snoring husband beside her, stale animosity crowding the room from all angles, smothering her wounded spirit. She had married Mitchell at age nineteen soon after becoming pregnant.

When Sharonda met Paris Downey, her friends told her she was crazy. Paris was known throughout the city. He was loud and boisterous. He had been to jail, and he didn't mind if people knew. When he spoke, people listened, and when he told bad jokes, they all laughed anyway. When they told her she was making a mistake, Sharonda knew her friends were just jealous. She could tell by the way they said it. When they spoke bad things about him, she could hear the titillation in their voices. She could see it on the grin that crept over their faces every time she talked about her rugged out-of-control man.

The truth of the matter is that Sharonda wasn't exactly sure when they had become an item. She met Paris at a club one night; they went out for breakfast afterwards. The next night they went out to dinner, and she had been seeing him ever since. Before long, Paris helped her to obtain an apartment. The day after she moved in, he showed up with furniture. She had no idea where it came from. She remembers the day very clearly because the relationship would be permanently altered before nightfall.

There was a brown vinyl couch and loveseat that clearly were used. They were accompanied by two white lamps that were much too big for where they were to be placed, and a round oak coffee table that was too low to the ground to be useful. It was at this point that Sharonda first began to wonder what type of situation she might be dealing with. It was not the pace of the courtship that bothered her; it was the disregard for her opinion. She had seen June Atkins become marginalized time and time again over the years. She was not June; she could never be June. Sharonda didn't want to appear unappreciative, but this was certainly not what she had envisioned for her first apartment.

"Where did you get this stuff? You could have let me see it before you started moving it in."

"What! You better be happy and stop trippin'! You could be sittin' on the floor watching the wall if you wanna be real about it!"

"It doesn't even match! Where did it come from anyway?"

At that point Paris put down the lamp he had been maneuvering and turned his full attention to Sharonda.

"Did you pay for this apartment? Your ass would still be at your momma's house if it weren't for me! Now you got the nerve to be complaining about the furniture! You need to shut your ass up and bring in them cushions off that truck! You hear what I'm saying?"

Sharonda stood staring him down. Her blood ran cold, and she imagined herself slapping him across the face. Never had she allowed a boyfriend to disrespect her in any way. Should she just leave him with this empty apartment? Right this second, just walk right out! She considered whether she should pack a bag or come back and get it later. Maybe she should wait until he left and then leave a cruel note for him. Before she could take her plans any further, she remembered why she had agreed to move here in the first place. It was time for her to be out of her mother's house. The relationship between Sharonda and her mom had been stretched to the absolute limit. Now the thought of returning home was her sole alternative. She couldn't go home; she had only been gone for a couple of days. If she was in need of her feeble mom after being gone for only two days, it wouldn't say much for a so-called independent young woman.

"What you waitin' for? Hurry up and get them damn cushions so we can sit down!"

All of Paris's friends stood watching, waiting to see if the argument would be carried further or if their mentor had once again given them a lesson on being the king of his castle.

Sharonda looked down and closed her eyes. She then turned and went to get the cushions.

Later that evening after Paris and his moving crew had left, she cried. She didn't cry because of his disregard for her feelings. She didn't even cry over the possible demise of their relationship. She cried tears of anger, anger that she hadn't stood up, anger that she didn't walk out, anger that she wasn't courageous enough to stand her ground come what may. She was angry that even now, as she lay curled up under the sheets, she hadn't gone somewhere far away to laugh and reiterate to whoever would listen, what a fool Paris had been to speak to her the way he did.

Paris never moved into the apartment. He continued to live across town with his friend Cedric and his cousin April, but he did obtain a key. Paris and Sharonda never seemed to be as closely bonded after the day she received the furniture. She never felt the same way about his "bad boy" attraction, and he, in turn, was less concerned with her welfare than she had been accustomed to. He showed up at the apartment at his leisure, but before long she was able to predict the frequency and duration of his visits. By the time a year had passed, Paris had merely become a nuisance that she was willing to put up with to maintain her residence. Since his visits were becoming less and less frequent, she was not extremely bothered by her state of affairs.

Chapter 3

...as I prayed to you for the gift of chastity I had even pleaded, "grant me chastity and self control, but please not yet." I was afraid that you might hear me immediately and heal me forthwith of the morbid lust which I was more anxious to satisfy than to snuff out.

St. Augustine

The first person Joseph looked for was Darrel Connely. He had met Darrel four months ago when Joseph and his dad had first come down to Texas to look over the campus. Darrel was starting his second year, and he seemed to be a pretty okay guy. But he was not to be found. What did turn up in the search was a world that Joseph had not discovered on his previous visit to the school.

As he walked across the tree-lined campus he found himself less on a search than on a tour of his new home. The buildings were gray and massive, but outlined with beautiful green manicured lawns and bright-colored flowers. Some kids rushing by obviously late for something important, a couple enjoying a cup of coffee. He couldn't help feeling overwhelmed just watching all of the young men and women, walking, talking, reading, or just enjoying the sunshine. There was energy in this place, a type of energy he had never experienced before. Just the idea that all of these students were doing as they pleased. It was all too clear just from the bounce in their strides and the conviction in their voices that these people were decision-making, self-assured adults. He couldn't help relating their assuredness to himself.

"Man, I'm really an adult now."

The freedom felt bittersweet. Like nearly all freshman away from home, Joseph had long awaited the power to make his own decisions. He believed strongly that he had the maturity and brains to manage his own affairs. But still, on the other hand, the academic hurdles that awaited him lowered his level of confidence and put a brake on his concern for future accolades. High school had been a breeze for the young man, but as so many friends and family members had told him in the recent past, *this* was the big time.

Joseph took to college well. He swiftly learned the important things necessary to get by socially in his new environment and, for now at least, that was his main goal—to get by. His personality seemed to thrive in the college atmosphere. He and Darrel never seemed to hit it off the way he had imagined, but soon enough Joseph met the two guys who would become his closest college buddies. They were Daniel Busby and Jovan Edwards.

Each of these friends established a relationship with Joseph widely different from the other. Both Dan and Jovan were young men who would be considered more intelligent than their average cohorts, but each chose to use his mental gifts in entirely different ways. Dan was a young man with lofty goals already in place. He was the first Busby ever to attend college, and in his mind, that was to be just the beginning. He was one of the few freshman who was already certain of his major (Education), and he had a number of graduate schools already picked out. Dan knew that his being able to attend college was a privilege that many young men his age could not afford. He was obligated to make the most out of his opportunity, obligated to use his education to open doors. All this was apparent in his serious demeanor. It wasn't necessary for Dan to lay out his whole plan to those he had befriended; it was pretty clear from the moment you met him. He was also a big guy. Students who saw him walking around campus always assumed he was an athlete, probably a football player, but when they met him, the contradictory manner was always a shock, especially to Jovan.

Jovan was the opportunist. He had met Dan through Joseph, and swiftly began to prod and needle the soft-spoken Southerner about his idealistic outlook. The quick-witted Jovan often verbally harassed "Buzz," as he nicknamed him, so badly that Dan began avoiding Jovan whenever possible. When sparing Buzz in favor of less familiar targets, Jovan often allowed his savage criticisms to get him into trouble that even his thousand dollar smile and glossy green eyes couldn't get him out of. Still, something about him was magnetic. His lust for life may not have been grounded in anything remotely honorable or upstanding, but his absolute candor was exciting.

Of the three young men, Buzz was the only one with a car. This fact did not seem to deter the other two from using the '85 Nissan Sentra as an intense focus for put-downs. Especially when the two perpetual passengers first realized that there was a small hole about the size of a silver dollar in the floor of the back seat that actually allowed the traveler to see through to the ground below. The two often suggested that Buzz used the hole to carry out various outlandish plans, such as looking up the skirts of unsuspecting female passengers or compromising their frequent nationalistic ramblings with spies from various right-wing organizations. Buzz, ever the diplomat, took it all with a smile.

College was good, or at least what college provided was good—freedom—and Joseph made the most of his. He rarely passed up an opportunity to hang with the fellas all night, or to sleep in all day. He, Jovan, and a reluctant Buzz made it a habit of clubbing around both Friday and Saturday nights. They often chose places on the far side of town, away from the college crowds because, in their opinion, college girls were too stuck up. The real horses were across town in the hood, "horses" because of the big rear ends that were always essential for a catch. Joseph had always been somewhat shy around women, but with Jovan at his side he had less of a problem approaching them, and he soon found that he wasn't bad at wooing the ladies. The days after school were often spent in each other's apartments, talking on the phone to ladies they had met on the weekend, unless they could talk Buzz into driving them across town where the current girls usually resided.

On one particular Saturday night Joseph caught sight of the girl he was certain was to change his life. As he and Buzz stood at the bar, he watched her. She was beautiful. From her captivating smile down to her shapely hips, there was not one cause for concern. Her hair was short and dark and framed her face beautifully. Her red lipstick accentuated her full lips, and surely drew the attention of more admirers than just Joseph. He could tell she was popular. It appeared she knew half the club personally, and for this reason he couldn't figure out why he hadn't seen her before.

He watched her dance, watched her chat with her friends, watched her walk. Unfortunately, all he could bring himself to do was watch. His feet turned to stone at the mere thought of approaching her, even though she had thrown more than one smile in his direction. There was a steady stream of acquaintances surrounding her. Joseph knew that any advances he made would be in front of an audience. It was a challenge he wasn't quite ready to tackle, so he decided that admiration from a distance would have to do.

Soon the lights were coming on and the club was emptying out. Joseph followed Jovan through the crowd toward the door, scanning the room for one last glimpse of his eye candy. He couldn't seem to find her. They came across Buzz calmly leaning against a wall. He had clearly been ready to go for some time. Jovan began asking Buzz about his night.

"Buzz, what's up, man? I saw you spittin' at the cutie in the purple skirt earlier. What happened to her?"

"Oh, she was cool. We talked for a while, but she left with her friends about thirty or forty minutes ago."

"Well, what's up? Did you at least get the number?"

"Yeah, I got her number. She stays down off of 40ᵗʰ."

Jovan glanced at Joseph, who was cutting a wry smile as he continued the conversation.

"Yeah, you better not lose that number. Honey's gonna treat you right when you hook up with her. You know what I'm saying."

"Why you say that? You know her?"

"Nah, I don't know her, but I see her up in the club all the time hollering at brothas. That's one of them Sunday morning babes, you know."

"Sunday morning? What, is she a church girl?"

"Nah, she ain't no church girl! A Sunday morning honey. You ain't never heard of a Sunday morning girl?"

"Jovan, what the hell is a Sunday morning girl?"

Jovan then turned to Joseph. "J, he ain't never heard of a Sunday morning girl. Will you please tell this brotha what a Sunday morning girl is?"

Joseph, smiling, walked up to Buzz, puts his arm around him, and began singing in a horribly out-of-tune voice: "The girl is EASAAAY."

Jovan joined in the next verse. "She's easy like Sunday morninnnnnnn."

Buzz shook his head in disgust and remarked, "Man, shut up! Ya'll ain't never seen that girl before! I don't know why either one of you is talking anyway, all the skeezers ya'll be tryin to hook up with."

Jovan then took the song into a more intense tone, screeching out another line loud enough for the people around them to hear.

"I said she's EASAAAAY!" Then he finished by softly singing the words closely into Buzz's ear, carrying the last word for nearly ten seconds. "She's easy like Sunday Mooo ohhhhh ooh ooh ninnnnn."

Buzz gently shoved Jovan away and proceeded toward the car, irritated with the spectacle his friends had made. The crowd was still filing out of the club and people close by were giggling at the joke.

Suddenly, out of the rumbling of chatter around him, a low voice spoke closely into Joseph's ear. "So what's up, you must got a girl since you can't come and talk to me."

Joseph turned and realized that it was indeed her, his "dream-girl," but even though it seemed obvious, he wasn't quite sure that she was actually talking to him. The most embarrassing thing he could do would be to reply to an advance that was directed at someone else. He paused, wondering if he should answer her question, or simply ask whether she was talking to him or to someone else. Before he could respond, she concentrated her stare directly on him:

"Helloooo, you can't talk to a sista?"

Joseph tried to speak in the calmest tone possible, but the smile on his face gave away his immediate excitement. "Oh, I'm sorry, I didn't know you were talking to me. What did you say, do I have a girl?"

"I said you must have a girl, cause I know you saw me looking and you straight ignored me."

He was nervous. She looked even better with the lights on than she did before.

Despite their low tones, he knew all of her friends could hear the conversation, and so could Jovan. Over and over again, all Joseph could think to himself was, *Don't screw this up. Please don't screw this up.*

"Nah, it's not that I got a girl. You was just hangin' with your friends so tight you didn't look like you was looking to meet nobody, so I figured I would just let you do your thing, you know."

She smiled and responded, "Well I might want to meet somebody if they're the right somebody. I don't know, are you looking to meet anybody?"

Joseph responded quickly, "No I'm not looking to meet anybody, I'm looking to meet you." His smile was growing wider, but by now he didn't care.

"Oh excuse me. You looking to meet me, huh? And why exactly do you want to meet me?"

"Cause tonight is your lucky night."

The statement was far cockier than Joseph intended, but it was the first thing that he could think of. He stood there holding his breath, hoping that she wouldn't laugh or embarrass him. He heard her friends giggle and mutter to one another.

"I heard that! Sharonda, this is your lucky night, girl!"

After sharing in their revelry, she turned back to Joseph. "My lucky night, huh? We'll see about that with your pretty eyes. You look like one of them college boys. Ain't you on the wrong side of town?"

Joseph was blushing. He often received compliments on his eyes, but none drew the response this one did. "What? You got a problem with college boys? Don't knock it until you've tried it. I've learned a whole lot of stuff."

Joseph could hear Jovan and Buzz, who had now returned to see what the hold up was, chatting back and forth behind him but he couldn't make out what they were saying. He didn't much care at the moment, as his full attention was focused on the captivating woman in front of him.

Sharonda responded, "Yeah, well maybe you can teach me something? I never could manage to pass biology. You know anything about biology?"

"For you, I might decide to major in it. You know, go to grad school and all that."

The two carried their discussion back and forth into the parking lot, and to his glee, they soon began speaking on the phone daily. She was by far the most attractive woman he had ever found the favor of in all his nineteen years.

Her name was Sharonda Atkins, and she was four years Joseph's senior. She worked part-time at the mall across town. Sharonda was not one to hold her tongue, and their conversations quickly grew intense. She said what was on her mind, and he ate it up. She told him that, although she had a boyfriend, she just couldn't resist approaching him, and that he was physically what she wanted in a man. He told her that a boyfriend was nothing to him, and it would take a lot more than that to scare him off.

The two began seeing each other regularly, and the relationship began to evolve, but only to a certain point. Sharonda was very removed in many ways, and she never allowed Joseph to get very close to her personally. She kept the relationship at a safe distance that always seemed a little too safe for Joseph. They spent most days together in her apartment. They shared little with each other about their hopes and dreams, or even their plans for next week. It was merely a simple bond that one was intent on maintaining and the other was willing to settle for.

Chapter 4

God created man because he was disappointed with the monkey.
Mark Twain

While squandering his time away in an afternoon philosophy class, Joseph caught sight of both Buzz and Jovan standing outside the room. They were motioning for him to come out, but he pointed at his watch and tried to let them know—

"Five minutes."

This was a teacher who didn't take kindly to people strolling out of his classroom early. They folded their arms and leaned against the hall wall. It wasn't too often that both his comrades tracked him down in the middle of the day on campus. He pondered what might be the reason for the unusual visit.

"Maybe they want to make a run to the field to check out the track meet. That would be cool, but I don't know if I can miss another English Lit class again; that would be like the third or fourth time this month."

He sighed and shrugged his shoulders as his two cronies continued to motion for him to abandon the class and come to them. Finally, after numerous hand gestures back and forth, the class was over, and Joseph was first out the door. His decision was made.

"I know I got at least a strong C coming in English Lit, besides this might be the last meet we have at home this season."

But to his surprise, the track meet was not on today's agenda. Jovan hurriedly began questioning his buddy. "Man, what's the name of that dude Sharonda says she's seeing?"

Joseph was caught off guard with the question. "What? I don't know, something whack like London or Rome or something."

Buzz jumped into the conversation. "Is his name Paris?"

"Yeah, that's the sucker's name. Why, what's up?"

Joseph began walking in the direction of his next class, offhandedly suggesting that whatever it was his two friends were so worked up about wasn't going to worry him.

Buzz countered Joseph's remarks in a tone that wasn't customary for his soft-spoken friend. "Man, dude is for real! She didn't tell you that fool is crazy? Joseph, you my boy, and I'm trying to let you know right now, you and Jovan ain't from around here, but I am. Folks around here know the name Paris Downey. The fool is straight 51/50."

Joseph maintained his nonchalant demeanor. "Man, what are y'all talking about? She told me dude was always trying to be some fake gangsta. I ain't even trippin' off him. And besides, it ain't like she's gonna tell him. She wants to keep everything on the under just like I do."

Jovan spoke up. "Fake gangsta! Man, Buzz's cousin said that brother smoked a fool three years ago!"

Joseph stopped walking as Jovan continued. "And on top of that, he did time for selling D, and for burglary. This ain't no fake gangsta. This is a straight lunatic!"

"Sharonda said he did time, but she didn't mention nothing about him killing nobody."

Jovan then offered what was, in his eyes, the only sensible answer:

"Well, of course not, not if she wants to see your ass again. Damn, man, that's probably why she got with a brother from out of town anyway. She knew you wouldn't know about that crazy fool she been hanging with."

Buzz agreed. "Ain't nobody from around here gonna risk they

damn neck going out with Paris's lady."

Joseph spent most of the rest of that day sitting in his room. He played some video games and listened to some CDs, but in his mind, what he was really doing, was aimlessly roving about his consciousness, deciding to do this, and then to do that. He knew what would be the sensible thing to do. He kept hearing his father's voice telling him, "You got too many wants and you don't know your needs."

Still, Joseph couldn't believe that Sharonda would actually continue to see him if she felt his life were in danger. His mind kept coming to her defense.

"She's got to be tired of a guy like that, anyway. She probably just sees in me a chance to spend some time with a guy that knows how to treat a woman. Why shouldn't she be able to have that? Hell, if there's one thing I know, it's that she definitely falls into the category of both wants and needs."

Joseph decided to call her and casually ask if she had been completely on the level about her "other friend," as she often referred to him.

Sharonda appeared to not be at all surprised on the phone.

"Yeah, folks always saying Paris did this and Paris did that, but he didn't kill nobody. I bet your friends didn't tell you that the police arrested somebody else for killing the dude that he supposedly shot."

She assured Joseph that, although he had been involved in some illegal activity, Paris was not a maniac. "He just goes around playing this hard-core role."

And anyway, it's not like she would tell him that she was seeing someone else. As long as they didn't flaunt their relationship all over the place it didn't really matter. Joseph forced himself to support her case and, in spite of the protests of his two closest confidants, the two continued to spend time together.

With finals fast approaching, Joseph assured his sister Jasmine that he would be bringing home nothing but top-notch grades. She, in turn, reminded him of what he needed to do to be awarded the family vehicle in less than a year. But after hanging up the phone, he sighed, and considered the fact that the family car couldn't possibly offer the gratification of what lay across town awaiting his company that evening.

He had agreed to pick up a video on the way over to Sharonda's apartment that night. Now, all he was waiting for was the ever-reliable Buzz to give him a lift. Everything went cool, as usual. Sharonda opted not to cook that night, so they had some Burger King to munch on, but that was more than okay with Joseph. The video was good, but the massage later on was even better. Now it was getting late, and they relaxed, lying on the couch listening to slow music and talking about whatever it was that came to mind. From the night they met…to old flames that they weren't proud of…to getting spanked with extension cords as children. There was more discussion and laughter than was typical of their nights together. As he listened to her giggle and chat about silly escapades of the past, he heard vehicles pull up or pull out of the apartments every now and then.

Sharonda, reminiscing, said, "I remember my dad actually spanked me with a piece of beef jerky one time just because I broke the knob off the TV set."

"Are you serious?"

"Yeah, you know I don't like beef jerky to this day! Why is it always just one of the parents that does all the spanking? All my friends would be talking about their mothers whooping them all the time but it was always my father who got me—when he was around at least. Who did the spanking in your house?"

"My dad, same as you. My pops didn't play. If I gave him a reason to, he would whoop me today, and I'm a grown man. He never whooped my sister though. She got away with murder!"

"I bet your mom never whooped you though, huh?"

"My moms? Nah, she never whooped me! I was her baby. Moms had a brother's back for real!"

"What happened to her?"

"She died in a car accident when I was nine."

"Oh, I'm sorry."

"It's cool. You know, that's how stuff goes sometimes. I still remember when my dad was telling me and my sister. Jasmine was like flipping out, screaming, and crying and whatever, you know. I just sat there looking at her. Looking back at that day, I don't really think I believed what he was saying, that my mom wasn't ever coming back. I was just thinking my dad and my sister both was crazy, you know what I mean? How could she not come back? She's my mother ain't she? Of course she's coming back."

"That must have been hard."

"Yeah, it was hard cause me and her was tight. I remember at the funeral service my dad read a poem. I always assumed he hated poetry. I don't know why. In all the nine years I had known him he just never seemed like the poetic type. When he was reading it I don't know if I was shocked at what the poem said or just at the fact that he had written one.

I once felt I had found the bottom
The darkest night one could surmise
But I had not yet endured the fate
Of premature goodbyes

At God's request may Satan test
The anchor of fragile lives
Heartfelt petitions for my Lord's sweet mercy
But no hint of heaven sent replies

The victim of violent attacks was I
The object of slander and lies
Neither at its worst could instill the pain
Of premature goodbyes

Sharonda, listening intently, responded to the poetry. "Damn! He was hurtin'! I would have been bawling my eyes out just from hearing the poem."

"I made it a point to remember that poem. He never read it again, but I found it written on a paper in his jacket pocket later that night. I didn't really understand it when I was nine, but for some reason I still felt the need to read it over and over again. I guess I figured if something could make my dad cry, it had to be important. I understand it now though. I know just what he was saying and how he was feeling, the same way I was feeling. I still have the paper I took from his jacket pocket. I pull it out and read it every now and then even though I know it by heart. But you're the first person I ever shared that poem with. It kind of feels a little strange saying it in front of somebody since I've been quietly saying it to myself all these years."

"I feel honored to have heard it. Something that means that much to you is nice to be able to share with someone else."

Sharonda considered the poem in her mind, the emotions that must have engulfed the person who wrote it. She then began reflecting on the poem's significance to her own life. Never in her past could she recall someone speaking poetry to her. The ability to use words in this way, to sharply yet honestly express one's sentiments, she found appealing. At once she recognized the parallel distinctions the poem presented to them both.

Joseph started to feel the pressure of tears against his eyes. He took a few seconds to gather himself before moving the focus of the conversation away from the funeral. "Me and pops are cool, but it ain't the same as it was with moms. He was always closer to my sister. But that's okay though. Me and him always had an understanding. As long as I kept my grades straight, and was at church on Sunday morning, he stayed off my case for the most part."

Sharonda then made a conscious attempt to lighten the discussion. "Well, I'm glad you kept your grades straight or you probably wouldn't have ended up here for me to meet you."

"What about *your* dad? Were you close to him?"

"Please! What dad? I see his ass every couple of years, and that's enough for me! That story about the beef jerky is one of only a few stories I have about my dad. It was pretty much just me and my mom from when I was seven until now."

"Damn, that's tough."

"Oh no, don't be sad! We were better off. At least I know I was better off. I think my mom would still take him back if he showed up with a dime and a nickel to share with her. I don't know why she always feels like she ain't no good unless she has a man in her life."

"Maybe she wanted him to be there for you?"

Then, as the two deliberated, the sound of one particular vehicle caused Sharonda to pause. After calmly suggesting she needed to stretch her legs, she casually went by the window to take a peek. In a flash, she turned to Joseph and shrieked, "Paris is outside!"

The fantasy was over, and the look and sound of great urgency was enough to tell Joseph that this matter was to be taken seriously. Sharonda's voice quickly went into a whisper, but at the same time lost none of its fervor.

"Go back into the laundry room and be quiet! Please don't let him see you here! Just be quiet and don't say nothing. He won't want to stay. Don't leave anything in here for him to find!"

Joseph didn't have time to think. He grabbed his shoes and his coat and headed for the back laundry room.

"Here, don't forget the champagne bottle!"

Sharonda ran to put the wine glasses in the cupboard and to grab her robe. Joseph took the bottle with him as he went into the back room. He pushed the door closed, but left a little crack so he could hear what was going on up front. About then, he heard the doorbell and a knock at the door almost simultaneously.

She yelled from her room, "Who is it?"

There was no answer. Joseph heard her briskly walk down the hall to the door and, in her most authentic voice state, "Oh, Paris, is that you? I didn't know you was coming by tonight."

A slow-talking male voice replied, "What's up, you ain't happy to see a brotha?"

Joseph looked around the room to see if there was anything he could use as a weapon. There was nothing but an old tattered broom. He hadn't left enough space in the doorway to get a decent look at the unannounced visitor and to see what type of physical adversary he would make. He racked his mind for anything that his good buddy

Buzz might have mentioned about this guy being big or small or carrying weapons or whatever, but he could come up with nothing. As he listened to the two dragging on a seemingly pointless conversation, Joseph began to think that the possibility was increasing that Paris would soon leave and things would be brought to order, but still he could feel his heart racing and his body tensing. He began to recite the prayer used by so many over-indulgers when they come to that time in their life that brings them face-to-face with all of their poor decisions:

"Lord, please just let me get through this. If I get through this, I won't ever see this woman again, I promise. I won't miss another class in my life. I won't even go clubbing again if you just help me right now."

As he continued listening to the conversation going on outside, he kept his eyes shut tightly and depended on a combination of prayer, hope, and meditation to somehow bring about good fortune. All the while, the dialogue in the front room continued. Now they were discussing how one of his friends wanted to date one of her friends. He wanted to set the date up between the two, but Sharonda suggested that his friends were no good, and it was not going to happen. Then Joseph heard him ask,

"You still got that jacket I left over here?"

She replied, "Yeah, it's in my room, I'll go get it."

The room was right next to where Joseph was hiding. He quickly angled his body so that he could see her as she walked by the door. Right behind her he saw Paris follow her into the bedroom. He only had a quick glance, but Joseph could tell that Paris was not a huge guy. His clothes were baggy, so it was difficult to tell how bulky he was. Now Joseph could hear their voices loud and clear. Paris was talking about Sharonda wearing his clothes and keeping them at her house.

"All these damn clothes you got up in this closet and you steadily trying to take my shit. This jacket hit me for $120. You could at least wash my shit after you take it."

The room was dark, but Joseph, now feeling around with his hand, found his weapon in the champagne bottle that he had set off to the side. He clutched the bottle, and desperately continued his confused, silent meditation in hopes that some cosmic force might hear and respond. He could feel the sweat in his palm, which allowed the bottle to easily slide around. His concentration grew so intense that it seemed to be making him dizzy. His breaths were getting shorter. Something inside was telling him to ready himself. Whatever was going to happen was going to happen now.

Just then he heard Paris' voice getting louder. "No telling what else of mine you got in here."

He was right outside the door. Joseph backed away just in time to see the door swinging open.

Paris was still talking. "What happened to my Raiders hat that you took out my car? You probably got a little stash where you hiding all my..."

Paris never even finished the sentence. As he flicked on the light switch, Paris began to turn in Joseph's direction. Things were moving in slow motion. Joseph swung before his mind could think. The bottle landed hard against the front of Paris' forehead. Glass exploded throughout the small room, so loud it was like a bomb going off. Paris' body fell against the dryer and onto the floor. The adrenaline continued to flow. Joseph started to kick him, but Sharonda ran in screaming,

"Stop, stop, you're gonna kill him!"

Joseph stopped and looked. Paris was down on the floor, not moving at all. He noticed that the injured man was even smaller than he had suspected. Paris' hair was long, and in disarray. There were trickles of blood on his face and on the ground. Glass was strewn about the floor.

"I gotta go," was all that could come to his mind. "I gotta go."

He grabbed his things and ran out of the house. All the while, Sharonda kept repeating, "I can't believe this, I can't believe this!"

Joseph ran until he was out of the apartment complex, and then he slowed to a hurried walk. The streets were as quiet as they were dark. But still, Joseph could hear his conscience as if it were being rewound and played over and over again through hundred-watt speakers. The crash of the bottle against the forehead, Sharonda's voice at a high, piercing pitch he had never heard before.

The monotonous thumps of his boots against the pavement and the deep heavy breaths he sucked in and out were the only sounds in his company. His eyes focused on the shadows cast down before him as he passed one streetlight after the other. Even the shadows, long and obscure, were convicting him. He continued on until he reached a corner store with a phone booth outside. He was now at least a mile from the occurrence, but as he dropped change into the phone, he still continued looking over his shoulder. Each ring brought more agony, with the possibility, "What if he doesn't answer?"

Buzz was not known to keep late hours, and since Joseph had suggested that he would likely stay all night at Sharonda's, Buzz had no reason to expect Joseph's call. By the sixth or seventh ring, he picked up.

"Buzz, you gotta come get me!"

Buzz, obviously half asleep, complained.

"Ah, man, I thought I wasn't picking you up until the morning."

"Buzz, this is for real, man. I just had it out with Paris."

As Joseph spoke, he realized that there was blood on his hand and right forearm. He hadn't felt any cuts, so he wasn't sure if the blood was his or not. Upon closer inspection, he realized that there had been a small shard of glass lodged in his hand near the base of his thumb. As he sat and waited for Buzz near the back of the store, he couldn't seem to get a good grip on the glass to get it out. For one thing, there was not much light where he sat, and even if there had been, he couldn't keep his hand from shaking so he could pull it out.

Buzz arrived quickly. He drove around the block once, but didn't see Joseph. After parking in the store parking lot for a few moments, he saw his friend finally appear from around the back, and Joseph quickly jumped into the car. Upon seeing the blood, Buzz asked in astonishment,

"What the hell happened?"

When Joseph told his friend about the wild events that had taken place, Buzz couldn't believe what he was hearing.

"I *told* you to leave her alone, I *told* you!"

Joseph asked Buzz to go into the store for him and grab a couple of Band-Aids, which Buzz did. Upon returning, Buzz asked what shape Paris was in when Joseph left the apartment. Joseph gave the best description he could manage.

"He was out cold, man. He looked like he was breathing, though. You can't kill somebody with a bottle, can you?"

The two continued on for over an hour after they got to Joseph's place. They went round and round with Joseph's muddled story, and Buzz's expressions of disbelief. Neither offered any comfort to the situation.

Chapter 5

I had once believed that we were all masters of our fate—that we could mould our lives into any form we pleased…I had overcome deafness and blindness sufficiently to be happy, and I supposed that anyone could come out victorious if he threw himself valiantly into life's struggle. But as I went more and more about the country I learned that I had spoken with assurance on a subject I knew little about…I learned that the power to rise in the world is not within reach of everyone.

Helen Keller

"The last time I cried… the last time I cried was because Paris pissed me off. Now I'm sitting here crying because I don't know if I should say I'm sorry or if I should find a way to kill his ass! I wish I never would've met him!"

"Say you're sorry? Come on, girl, you know you need to forget about that fool! I don't care what you did wrong. Ain't no man ever got the right to put his hands on you! Never!"

The left side of Sharonda's face was badly bruised. Her eye was nearly swollen shut. It was Jahlan, her oldest friend, who was there to drive her to and from the hospital. Jahlan was one friend that even though they didn't always agree, Sharonda knew was in her corner in times of trouble.

"Since you obviously ain't gonna just come out and tell me, I guess

I'm gonna have to ask you straight out. Did you tell them who did that to you? I know they had to ask."

"What's the point? He's gonna end up in jail anyway. He's too dumb not to."

"Sharonda, that's not the point! You need to stand up and make him pay for that shit! Look at you! You can't let no man put his hands on you like that!"

"Look, I already know the speech, okay. I heard people give it to my mom more than enough times! Just let me sleep on your couch for a few days and I'm gonna handle it my way."

"You better handle it some kind of way. I know you don't want me to have to put the J momma body slam on that fool!"

Sharonda mustered up a smile, but the relief that Jahlan offered in the form of mild humor didn't last long. Sharonda couldn't stop thinking about Joseph. In all likelihood she had seen him for the last time.

She thought about how different Joseph was from all the other guys she dated. He wasn't the first guy she saw behind Paris's back, but he was the only one that lasted. She had known of the potential danger for them both if Paris were to find out, and now she felt guilty for not being completely up-front with Joseph.

From the beginning, Sharonda thought that Joseph was a guy who might end up doing some good things in this messed up world, not because he was smart, and not because he was in college, but because he was one of the only truly unselfish honorable guys she had ever met. The way she saw it, he would probably be better off never seeing her again anyway.

It was very early. Sharonda glanced over at Jahlan, thinking how grateful she was to have a friend willing to be there for her, regardless of the circumstances. Then she stared out in front of her and watched the sun rising above the hills causing shimmering waves on the highway. The question that continued to haunt her was, *Why hadn't she given hers and Joseph's relationship a real chance?*

"Jahlan."

"What's up?"

"You think me and Joseph would've worked out if I had dropped Paris?"

"If you had dropped Paris? Damn, how would I know? You kept the boy so locked up in your apartment I hardly got a chance to meet him. I don't know if you was ever going to be able to get rid of Paris anyway. You know, he thinks once a woman is his, then she's always his. You should probably just look at this as your way to get away from that asshole."

"But what if I had never been with Paris and I met Joseph? Do you think it would have worked then?"

"You was seriously sweet on that boy, huh? Little college boy had you open, didn't he? I don't know. He seemed kind of young. It probably would have been some fireworks at the house when he brought your old butt home for the holidays, I'll tell you that."

"What you mean my old butt? I only had four years on him."

"I don't know, girl. I don't think you're gonna have to worry about that now anyway. You better hope Paris don't find him or won't nobody be going home for the holidays. You know what I'm saying?"

Sharonda's mind still drifted back to last night. Lying on the couch, cuddled up with Joseph, the stories they told, the soft kisses, the poem he shared, all seemed clearer to her than the violent episode that followed. Although he never said the words, she knew Joseph loved her. The way he called her every morning before class, and was always willing to alter his schedule to see her, spoke as loudly as words ever could. Even though he knew she had a boyfriend, he never once asked her to choose. He never once displayed any anxiety because of their need to sneak around.

In the past, she had always been able to gauge the time when a man's interest in her would begin to diminish. Usually not long after the first sexual encounter, the enthusiasm and chivalrous acts of her many admirers would begin to wane. Sharonda had become accustomed to cutting off relationships before they ever reached the stale, "What are we here for?" stage. But Joseph never seemed to fit the mold.

Getting comfortable on Jahlan's couch wasn't easy. It was lumpy, and she could feel the springs coming straight through the cushion. Besides that, she could only lay on her right side. When she tried to lay the left side of her face to the pillow, she could feel her cheekbone throbbing with pain.

The cushion smelled like a combination of dust and milk, likely from Jahlan's five-year-old spilling cereal as he watched morning cartoons. Sharonda envisioned her apartment—clean and freshly dusted. She always took pride in the neatness of her home. Even her mom was pleased on the infrequent visits she made. Although it was only a small day-bed, her bed was more comfortable than any she had ever slept in. The pillows were fluffy, the sheets were warm and crisp, and they always carried the scent of fabric softener. Visitors to her home knew that she always kept her apartment in the best condition.

The thought of returning home to her mother kept at her. She could hear the voice as if it were only inches from her ear: "I told you that you should have stayed home. I don't know what you were thinking, moving out to the other side of town. What did you do to anger him like that anyway? You've got to be more careful how you conduct yourself with men, Sharonda."

Her conflicted thoughts leaped from last night...to years into the future...to the milky smell of the couch. How could she live with herself were something to happen to Joseph, whose only real crime was falling for a woman who didn't deserve him in the first place? What would he do now? Would he stay in Texas? Would he go home to California and never come back? Maybe he would call the police. No, why would he do that when he's the one who hit Paris with the bottle. Maybe he'll drop out of school all together and never do anything with his life. It would be my fault if he dropped out of school and ended up working at some dead-end job making minimum wage for the rest of his life.

Sharonda looked at the telephone on the wall. Maybe she should call him? She could call just to make sure he was okay. She could let him know that Paris still doesn't know where he lives. For a second, it sounded like a good idea. But before she made a move toward the phone, she reconsidered. She imagined the disappointment in his voice. Why would he want to talk to me? He's probably sitting somewhere thinking how he was such a fool to be seeing me in the first place; how he wished he had never met me.

The springs in the couch were jabbing into her side. Sharonda longed to be in her apartment, lying in her own bed, watching her television. She got up and walked into the kitchen to find something to quench her thirst and hopefully alleviate the dusty taste in her mouth. On the refrigerator were numerous pieces of artwork done by five-year-old Julian. There was a photo of him on blue paper surrounded by seashells. Another was a drawing of two stick figures, obviously Julian and his mom standing in a row of flowers. A second drawing was of the same two stick figures standing under the yellow sun next to a big tree. The names on this picture—not clearly written across the top of the page— "Julian and Mommy." Sharonda knew who Julian's dad was. She knew he wasn't often around for his son. She knew that Julian would probably grow up having little or no relationship with his father.

Her mind flew back to her childhood.

Why are fathers so invisible? Why are they there one day and gone the next? Sharonda remembered the closeness she shared with her own dad when she was small. How she always took his side over her mom's. How could he just leave like that? A sharp pain shot through her bruised cheek when she tensed her face in disgust. She grabbed a glass from the cupboard and poured herself some juice. It was sweeter than the juice she drank at home. She wondered where Paris was at that moment.

I wonder what he would do if I went back to the apartment. He might not mind if I stayed there; I know he's not gonna want to move in there. He likes it too much where he's at. He's not gonna want to give up having that apartment to go hang out in when he feels like it. Ain't nobody else he can trust to look out for that place and keep it clean. Hell, I must be crazy thinking about going back there. He'd probably kill me on sight if I ran into him.

I hope Joseph knows enough to stay away from around there. Paris would leap over me ten times to get to him. Nah, I know Joseph ain't ever going there. Why would he? Our days was probably numbered anyway. He's a man just like the rest of them, college boy or not. Only difference, is he ain't got no kids to leave behind yet.

Chapter 6

Virtue, even attempted virtue, brings light; indulgence brings fog.
C. S. Lewis

The next day, Buzz showed up with valuable information. Paris was fine. He had gotten plenty of stitches and suffered a mild concussion, but that was the extent of the damage. Buzz also found out that Paris had more than interrogated Sharonda—she was beaten badly. Paris had found out from her that the name of the guy he was looking for was "Joseph," and that he was attending the local university. What he didn't know was what Joseph looked like. Surprisingly, Sharonda had no pictures.

Joseph had a mixed reaction to the news. He was glad Paris wasn't seriously injured, but how much did he have to fear? He began to work out plans in his head to make himself difficult to locate. Spring break was less than a month off. He would be going home for three weeks during break. Since he had a month-to-month lease, he could acquire a new apartment when he returned to school, stay out of the clubs he had frequented, and above all else, definitely stay away from Sharonda. The situation was looking plausible.

Joseph knew there was no way he could ever tell his dad, or even his sister Jasmine, for that matter. They would only overreact. What would be the point? The right thing was already being done. He would concentrate more on his studies, and less on women. Telling them this would only add more confusion to the predicament.

Joseph went about his new and improved daily routine with anxious dedication. He knew he was far behind where he should be in his classes. He was early to class and late out of study hall. Buzz enjoyed his friend's newfound commitment. Buzz had always been more comfortable in a study hall than in a smoke- filled club anyway. The only one left out in the cold was Jovan, who refused to give up his provocative lifestyle because of Joseph's misfortune. So it appeared the threesome was down to two.

Still, Joseph was very conscious of where he showed his face. He did not speak to Sharonda after the incident. Although he still felt some longing to see her, it was much easier to thwart those desires now that he knew he could possibly be risking his life by being with her. Buzz kept constant communication with his insider cousin, finding out just how heated things were. The ongoing reply was that Paris was keeping his eye out for that college boy.

One day, while heading to his car from his last class of the day, Buzz caught a glimpse of a red, late-model Mustang slowly cruising through the parking lot. There was no question in his mind who was in the vehicle. Buzz made a quick change of direction and stepped inside a department building. Paris didn't have a good description of Joseph, but he would have no trouble recognizing Buzz. Paris had hosted Buzz and his cousin at his apartment on more than one occasion. He also knew that Buzz and Joseph were acquaintances. Friends of Paris's had seen them together many times at the clubs. The Mustang continued passing through the parking lot, and soon disappeared. But the event prompted Buzz to wonder. It wouldn't be too difficult for Paris to track *him* down in an effort to get to Joseph. Paris probably wouldn't look to physically harm Buzz, since his cousin and Paris were friends, but who knew how bad he wanted to find Joseph? He might do anything. Something needed to be done.

The next day, while visiting Joseph's place, Buzz got his opportunity to take action. Joseph went to the laundry room to wash his clothes. Buzz picked up the telephone and used the speed dial that was listed on the front to call Jasmine. After a few moments of trying to explain to her who he was, he was able to get to the point of why he was calling.

"Um, Ms. Shaw, I think Joseph might be in some trouble. He doesn't know I'm calling you, and he would probably be pretty upset if he found out, but I think somebody out there needs to know what's happening."

"What do you mean he's in trouble? What kind of trouble?"

"Well he was seeing this girl out here you know, and she…"

"He's in trouble over a girl? He ain't got nobody pregnant out there, I know!"

"No, ain't nobody pregnant. What happened is that she kind of had a boyfriend."

"What? So he's out there fighting over some girl? Well, I hope he gets his butt kicked! It'll serve him right!"

"No, see, you don't understand. The guy who this girl was seeing is, like crazy. This fool don't fight; he kills folks."

"Well, what's going on? Are you saying that this guy is trying to kill my brother?"

"Well, I don't know? I think he might be."

For a moment it was obvious that, although she kept talking, Jasmine didn't know what to say or do. Her voice got louder as she called Joseph names, and even though she didn't know Sharonda's name yet, she called her names as well. When the conversation was over, she slammed the phone down hard. After standing there in the same place for a few moments and allowing the fury to subside, she sat down and quietly allowed a few tears to run down her face. She then did what she knew she had to do. She called her father and told him about the trouble his son was into.

Mr. Shaw didn't take the news well. He sat quietly as his daughter told him what she had found out. His face expressed disbelief. When she was done, he rose from his seat and walked into the kitchen. Jasmine didn't move. She knew that the conversation was not over. When he returned a moment later, he had a sealed can of peanuts, but just when he was about to peel the lid off he stopped, paused, and then asked, "Who is this Buzz kid? Did he sound like he was a close friend of Joseph's? I talk to the boy every week and I ain't never heard him mention no Buzz before."

Jasmine responded in a calm tone. "He said they'd been hanging out all the time since school started. He was at Joseph's apartment when he called. He said Joseph was outside doing laundry."

After a long sigh, Mr. Shaw continued. "He said this crazy fool is looking for Joseph, huh?"

Jasmine somberly responded, "I'm afraid so."

Jasmine's face hung down. She hated being the bearer of such wretched news.

Allen Shaw expected much from his son, and escapades of this type were not something that would be taken lightly. Even worse, they were not something that either of them expected from Joseph. They had both spoken to the young student on the phone many times, and never had he discussed anything other than how his studies were progressing. Mr. Shaw had always felt he had a very good relationship with his son. They had no problem talking together about the various things that most parents cringed at the thought of mentioning to their kids. Mr. Shaw assured his daughter that things would be alright, and that he would take care of the problem, but he was still worried. He couldn't believe his son would get himself into this type of situation, and furthermore, that he would not come to his father for help. A phone call would not be enough. Instead, he made plane reservations.

Even on the plane, Joseph's father stretched his brain in every conceivable direction trying to come up with the correct words to use in order to get through to his wayward son. He had no idea, until he sat down, how vital his window seat would turn out to be. Staring out into some of God's most wonderful creations allowed his mind to wander even deeper into the jumbled thoughts and reflections that kept at him. It was known to his neighbor within the first few seconds of his sitting down that there would be little or no conversation on this trek through the sky. When the gentleman's, "hellos" and "how are you's" were met with nothing more than grunts and nods, the hint was taken, and the gentleman made conversation elsewhere.

Mr. Shaw continued to wonder what he could have done differently in the past. He prayed for wisdom to handle the problem in the correct manner. His mind thought back to when Joseph's mom was still alive. Things would be so different if she were still in their lives. She was so patient, but at the same time she was strict. Joseph and his mom had such a connection that nothing could come between them, nothing other than death. Now here he sat, trying to replace her, and obviously failing miserably. Jasmine had always been closest to her father. She listened to what he taught her and she learned from his actions. Now she was a very successful real estate agent, and even more important, a dedicated Christian. But what about Joseph? He had always been a good kid. He always went to church, he always respected his father and his elders, but ever since his mom passed he had shown absolutely nothing in the way of mental fortitude. He remained content just blindly sauntering through life, with no major concern for anything. Mr. Shaw's own father had always taught his son that you've got to believe in something because, as the old saying goes, if you don't stand for something, you'll fall for anything. In the Shaw family, that something was God.

As Joseph's father refused the complimentary beverage with a wave of the hand, his thoughts continued to dominate him. *What can I do to get through to him? How can I show him how precious life really is, and how important it is to make good use of the few years God gives us on this planet.*

It was at that moment that he made a major decision, one that he knew his son wouldn't take lightly. Joseph would have to come home and attend school locally. He couldn't risk his son continuing on a path leading nowhere. Whatever was going to be done would have to be done while he and Jasmine played an active part in Joseph's life.

When Mr. Shaw arrived at Joseph's apartment, nobody was there. He went to the rental office and, using his overbearing personality, coerced the young man who was on duty to let him into the apartment to await his son. As he waited, he wandered around, gazing at what his son had accumulated at his residence. He tried to gain some inkling as to what was going on in his son's life. There were photos of a young woman on the mirror in his room. There were also framed photos both of the young lady and of Joseph's mom on top of his dresser. Inspecting Joseph's closet, he also noticed that the only picture of himself and Jasmine that Joseph had taken with him was in a bag in the closet, never unpacked. When Mr. Shaw grew tired, he sat on the couch and stared into nothingness.

Chapter 7

"Breathing in, I calm myself. Breathing out, I smile."
Thich Nhat Hanh

Daniel Busby sat on the trunk of his car listening to the radio. He had just left Joseph at the library on campus and was gassing up his Sentra before heading home. Then he caught sight of that same red Mustang he had seen cruising through the campus before. He stayed calm and made an attempt not to look in the direction of the car. When it continued on behind, Daniel squeezed his eyes shut and tried to tell himself that he had not been seen. He finished filling his tank, and replaced the nozzle on the pump, making an effort not to look up. He got into his car, but before he could turn on the engine he felt the red glare of a Mustang slowly pulling up beside him. He could see the bright color from the corner of his eye. He didn't look. Then a voice called out to him.

"Hey, Dan! Dan!"

Buzz's heart sank. His hands were clenched tightly around the steering wheel. There was nothing he could do but respond.

"What's up, Paris?"

"Say, man, I need to holla at you for a minute."

Buzz's mind was racing. *What can I tell him? He knows I know Joseph! I've got to tell him something!*

Paris got out of the car and walked up close to the passenger side window, even though he had been plenty close enough to hold a conversation from his own vehicle.

There was one guy in the passenger seat of the red muscle car who, for whatever reason, couldn't seem to stop grinning. His apparent happiness only worked to further the panic that already gripped Buzz. Paris leaned in and began to mutter small talk in a strangely low voice. He asked Dan how he was doing and how his cousin was doing. Then he said a couple of the usual things about just trying to get by and trying to get paid. As Buzz stared back he did his best to reciprocate, but his nerves gave him away, and he stumbled over his words.

Then Paris started in on him. "Yo, man, you know this cat named Joseph? He goes to your school?"

All Buzz could think of was not to let him know where Joseph lived. Buzz figured he could give out anything else without hurting his friend, as long as he didn't give out the phone number and address. Buzz replied, "Yeah, I know who he is. I think he's a business major."

"A business major huh? Well, you know, I got some *business* to handle with the dude. You know where I might be able to catch up, partner?"

"Damn, I don't know. He used to stay on campus, but I think he might have gotten his own spot somewhere."

"Yeah, that's cool, but you know, a couple of my folks say they saw y'all hanging at the club a few weeks ago, and that dude was your dog, you know what I'm saying?"

"Yeah, man, we rolled for a while, but we ain't all tight like that. We just kick it every now and then."

Then Paris looked around as if to check to see if anybody was paying attention to the conversation taking place. He bent his knees, squatted down low to the door, and continued talking. "Look, man, I'm gonna tell you like this. I ain't got no beef with you. You're family with one of my boys, so I'm gonna do my best to keep you out of this shit. But this shit can get ugly real quick, you know what I'm saying? I don't know where you live, and I don't want to know, but if I need to find out I can! So I'm telling you, dude, if you don't come correct right fucking now, the next time you see me I'm gonna be packing for your ass! What you need to do is come up off this information so you can be out of this shit!"

Buzz's thoughts sank to the pit of his stomach and he turned to stone. He couldn't think of anything except to make a plea on his friend's behalf. "Look, man, he didn't know she was your girl. I didn't even know. If I had known, I would have told him to stay away from her. He ain't from around here."

"Yeah, I know you didn't know cause if I thought you did know I wouldn't have come up to you talking, I would have come up banging, but as for your partner, it's too late for all that. We're gonna settle this real soon. So you got some info for me, or do you want to join your homeboy on my list?"

He was calling Buzz's bluff, and now the stakes were too high. Paris finally got the information he was looking for. As he walked away he smiled, and spoke back to Buzz: "Tell your cousin to call me so we can hook up," as if all that had just taken place were not all that important.

Buzz sat in his seat for a moment after the Mustang had pulled away, half hating himself and half happy to be unharmed. Then the urgency hit him, and he rushed to the phone booth to call his friend and let him know what had happened.

When Joseph walked into his apartment he heard his father's voice call him, and for a second he was astonished: First, that there was an intruder. Second, that it was his father.

"Dad? What are you doing here?"

Allen Shaw walked over to his son, and simply asked, "You don't have a hug for your old dad?"

After a token embrace, Mr. Shaw asked his son to sit and talk with him. He decided not to tiptoe around the reason for the surprise visit, but to come right out and get everything on the table. "I know you're into some trouble and I came out here to talk to you about it."

"What are you talking about? What kind of trouble?"

"This guy that's looking for you over some girl you're seeing."

"What have you been doing, spying on me or something? You

have no right to be all in my business like this! I'm a grown man!"

Mr. Shaw took exception to Joseph's tone as well as his words. He stepped nose to nose with his son and responded with equal hostility. "Boy, don't you ever raise your voice to me! I don't care if you're in DeAngeles, Texas or Timbuktu! If I have to put my hands on you, believe me I'm gonna make it count! You ain't grown enough yet to raise your voice to me, you hear me!"

Joseph stopped to think. He breathed in deeply in an attempt to calm himself. After brief but careful consideration he realized he would not win a shouting match. He stepped away and took a seat on the couch. "Look, Dad, I don't know how you know about this, but it ain't that big of a deal. I can handle my own problems."

"Well, why don't you tell me exactly what the situation is, and then we can decide if you can handle it or not."

Joseph let out a big sigh. He didn't want to tell his father the whole truth, but he didn't know how much he already knew. "Look, I'm telling you it's not that big a deal. I'm nineteen years old; I can take care of myself. How did you find out about Sharonda anyway?"

"Oh, is that her name, Sharonda? Well, she's a pretty young lady. I saw the pictures. I can see why you would be hesitant to let her get away, but apparently a friend of yours seems to think that this thing is a little bit more serious than you're telling me."

"Well, I'm not seeing her anymore, so it's done."

"Well, from what I was told, she isn't the one who's posing the threat. Now, are you going to tell me what happened, or am I going to have to stand here and continue to pull it out of you?"

Joseph was holding his head in his hands. His dad obviously knew much more than he had hoped.

"Fine! I met this girl who had a boyfriend. We started going out and one night when I was at her house the dude showed up. I didn't want to fight the guy so I went in the back and hid, just to keep the peace, you know? But dude had to go looking around the house for whatever reason. I don't know what he was looking for—clothes or something. Anyway, dude saw me, so I hit him in the head with a bottle and I left."

"You hit the boy with a bottle?"

"Well, what was I supposed to do? I didn't know how big he was, or if he had a weapon, or what he was gonna do!"

"You could've killed that boy! Oh my goodness, Joseph, I can't believe you did something like this!"

All the controlled, calm discussions that Joseph's father had envisioned while on the plane were fading away as his disbelief and anger continued to mount. Before long, the two were in an all-out shouting match. Mr. Shaw's temper grew more and more inflamed until he reached a point where he felt no more guilt over telling his son that he would have to return home to continue his schooling.

When the demand hit Joseph, it had a sobering effect. His voice quickly leveled out, losing its anger and gaining sincerity.

"Dad, you can't be serious."

"Do I look like I'm joking to you?" Mr. Shaw's voice, on the other hand, lost none of its ferocity. "Start packing your stuff up, because after this semester is over, you are coming home!"

"Dad you're making too big of a deal out of this. This ain't nothing. She was the finest girl in the world and I quit seeing her just like that. If nothing can convince you that I'm serious about studying hard, that should. I can get back into—"

But before he could continue he was made aware that the decision was non-debatable.

"I don't want to hear another word from you! You've been down here wasting your time and my money! Aside from that, you've even managed to put your own damn life in danger! I knew you were going to stretch your legs a little when you got out here, but I always thought you had a little more sense than to get caught up in something like this. You're coming home, and I don't want to hear another word about it. Now, pack up some stuff that you're not going to need for the next couple of weeks so I can take it home tomorrow! When the semester is over, you can come home with the rest of it, or you can sell it, or you can do whatever you want to do with it, I don't care!"

Joseph knew that to continue the discussion would be senseless. With one more sigh, he turned, walked into the next room, and began throwing some small knickknacks into a bag. All the while, his father intermittently hurled hostile comments down the hall at his son.

"Some aspiring gangster trying to hunt you down like a dog, and you're talking about it ain't no big deal! You're lucky your friend was worried enough about you to call somebody, no telling what might have ended up happening! And Lena Horne is the finest woman in the world, but I guess you wouldn't know nothing about that, being all young and stupid as you are! Got too many wants and don't know your needs, I'm telling you, that's what your problem is!"

As Allen Shaw, Jr. continued to mumble harsh words to himself about his half-witted son, he picked up the phone and dialed the airline to confirm his return flight and to ask about how much baggage he would be allowed to check onto the flight. As he sat on hold, he could hear the phone continuously clicking, which only irritated him more. He continued to shout down the hall at his son. "Boy, somebody trying to call in on this phone, probably one of these good-for-nothing women you done met down here! Whoever it is will just have to wait until I'm done!"

Joseph chose not to reply. An answer at this point would only serve as fuel to the towering inferno of outrage that was evident in his dad's voice.

As he continued to call over and over and to get no answer, Buzz grew more and more worried. He knew that his friend should be home. The two had just left each other not more than two hours ago. Where was Joseph? Why wasn't he answering the phone? Buzz chose to ignore the older woman standing only a couple of feet away, waiting to use the payphone. The woman was tapping her foot and folding her arms, clearly agitated at his continuous hanging up, then picking up the receiver and dialing again. He talked out loud to himself, "Come on, man, pick up the phone! What the hell are you doing? Pick up the phone!"

But his persistence was not rewarded. The phone continued to ring, and his anxiety continued to grow. Finally, he gave up hope of reaching Joseph on the phone and sped off in his vehicle toward Joseph's apartment.

Allen Shaw finally found it within himself to cease his vocal battery of his son and to sit quietly on the couch, waiting on hold for the airline operator to return to the phone. Joseph came into the room, dropped a bag onto the floor, then turned around and headed back down the hall. The shouting and hostility that had filled the apartment had now turned to silence. Mr. Shaw was short with the agent when she returned to the phone, but not rude. Without clearly saying so, he let her know that he did not appreciate the time he spent waiting for her on the phone.

As soon as he hung up the phone, he heard a knock on the door— just more things he was not in the mood to deal with. For a moment he sat on the couch and sighed, as if ignoring the knock might make it go away, but it came again. This time, he pulled himself up off the couch and, grumbling, went toward the door. His greeting to the visitor was in a voice that came across as far less than hospitable.

"Yeah, can I help you?"

The visitor replied in a calm, polite tone, "Is Joseph around?"

Mr. Shaw informed the young man that Joseph would be a minute, and then took a few steps toward Joseph's room to call him. "Say, Joseph, you got a friend out here at the door. Maybe you can get him to help you pack your stuff."

As Joseph emerged from his room, his father headed toward his seat on the couch. When Joseph turned the corner toward the doorway, his eyes locked onto Paris and his body froze. He stood for a second, quiet. Staring. Paris stared back. Not moving. Mr. Shaw turned and called to Joseph,

"Ah, is this that boy, Buzz, that called Jasmine on the phone?"

Joseph didn't reply. Paris kind of gave a half smile toward his prey. Mr. Shaw continued to question his son. "Joseph, you hear me talking to you?"

Then Paris suddenly reached into his coat and pulled out a handgun. Joseph turned, and started to run back down the hallway. When Mr. Shaw saw the commotion start, he didn't see the gun. He just saw his son turn and run in the other direction. So he ran toward Joseph. Shots rang out, but Joseph continued to run. His father reached him, and began pushing him down the hall and into the room. More shots were fired. Joseph ran to open the window in an effort to jump out, but soon realized that he would never be able to open it in time. He turned and looked at the doorway to see if Paris was coming, but what he saw was not an enraged Paris with a gun. What he saw was his father lying on the ground face up, his face grimacing. There was blood coming from his stomach. Joseph ran to him. He looked down the hall. Paris was nowhere to be seen. He knelt down to his father and opened his mouth, but no words came forth. Only moans, shouts of distress from Joseph.

Mr. Shaw was quiet. He appeared to be breathing, but his eyes were shut and his body was still. Joseph ran to the phone and dialed 911. As he talked to the emergency operator he continued to kneel at his father's side and put his arms around him. When Buzz arrived, the scene was bedlam. There were sirens all over. When he found his friend, Joseph, still in a bit of a trance, he didn't ask what happened. He didn't ask anything. Joseph just continued to mumble, "My dad is gone—he's gone."

The two hugged, and Buzz shared in his friend's misery. It was a night that neither minded being seen crying.

Chapter 8

I have been slowly recovering...from the general disease of my life.
Samuel Johnson

The Shaw family didn't take the loss well. Allen Shaw, Jr. had been a much-loved man. At the church, on the job, at home, most people felt the same way about him. He was God-fearing; he was honest, and he was a dedicated father. All of these things caused Joseph to feel even more guilt. He knew many people would see him as the no-good son who cost his father his life, and, in his own opinion, he deserved the judgment.

Joseph moved home right away, before the end of the semester. It was the least he could do under the circumstances, but the real friction came when he made it clear that he would not be attending the funeral. Jasmine let him know that this was unacceptable. Joseph would be embarrassed to be in the presence of the outpouring of love that would no doubt be shown at the services. He didn't want to attend the funeral as the villain who had caused the death of such a great man. He didn't even deserve to be allowed inside.

Jasmine was the only person Joseph told his feelings to. It wasn't until she realized his sentiment was sincere that she tried to console him. She initially held him accountable for her father's death. It was only a couple of days before the funeral that she set aside her sorrow and decided to take a chance at repairing what was left of her brother's broken spirit. But she couldn't get through, and soon lost her patience. Allen Shaw, Sr. had no words for his grandson. Theirs was known to be a relationship like no other, but this event had scarred it apparently beyond repair. Joseph knew, through his sister, how disappointed his grandfather was in him. His grandmother made attempts to call and suggest that it wasn't so very bad.

"Your grandfather just needs time to get over the shock. He'll come around." But Joseph had no hopes of that happening.

Joseph received a call from Buzz on a gloomy Wednesday afternoon. Just the fact that he was home at all at one o'clock on Wednesday afternoon led Buzz to assume that things weren't going all too well with his friend. But he had great news that he was sure would make a difference. Buzz told Joseph that Paris Downey had been captured by police in the very same neighborhood where he had committed the crime. Even better, he had been caught in possession of the same type of gun that was used in the killing.

"This idiot is never going to see the light of day once they prove it was the same gun. I'll bet you don't even have to testify they have so much stuff on him."

What appeared to be wonderful news to Buzz failed to lift the spirits of his downcast buddy. Joseph responded simply, "I hope he gets a damn needle in his arm." That was it. Joseph refused to join in with his friend in delighting over all the cruelties that lay in store for Mr. Downey. It was clear that his heavy burden had not been lifted. Joseph then changed the subject. He worked to make small talk for a short time, then politely excused himself from the phone with an apology, "I got to get back to cleaning the yard."

As the day of the funeral grew closer, Joseph's depression only grew stronger. Jasmine invited him to stay with her and her family for a while, but he refused. He didn't want to see family, and didn't feel that they much wanted to see him. He stayed in his father's house, which served as even more of a discouragement.

His days became less meaningful and his nights grew longer. He was sleeping less and less. Sitting up in his bed reliving the dreadful night, then falling asleep, and again reliving the dreadful night. He couldn't get away from it. Crying didn't help. Driving didn't help. Not even praying helped to relieve this agony, which stayed with him every second of the day. When some strange occurrence did allow him to laugh, he felt guilty. Nothing he ever experienced had been so real as the guilt that now haunted him. Never had anything rendered him so unable to deal with his own feelings. His sorrow now mastered him; his control was lost.

On the day of the funeral, Joseph could not be coaxed to attend. He began the day with a firm notion to sit at home and not leave his room. The more he tried to think of nothing, the more he grew furious at his thoughts, which were gravitating toward what he despaired. Soon he was on the road driving to nowhere, although driving was on the list of his many failed antidotes to misery. As he drove, he pictured what the funeral would be like. Hundreds, or even thousands, of people sitting in awe of Allen Shaw, Jr. Joseph's grandparents in the front, accompanied by Jasmine and her family. Then all of the aunts, uncles, nieces, nephews, and cousins gathered to pay their respects. The choir singing some slow, sad song causing everybody to cry even louder than they had before. Then Pastor Louis Wendell stepping up to the podium and giving a moving eulogy about a close friend of his whom God took sooner than anybody had expected. Then people would go up one by one and give personal testimonies about what a wonderful man he was. With every testimony, with every amen, with every tear that fell, would be the thought somewhere in the building of what type of son could have allowed this to happen to such a wonderful man.

Joseph continued to drive. The music on the radio played on and on, although he paid no attention to it. He was now hours away from home on a road that he had been on less than a handful of times. He was not lost, but he was in a place just unfamiliar enough to cause most people to take notice of the changed surroundings. However, Joseph didn't notice. His mind was still elsewhere. He didn't notice the sun slowly dropping behind the hills, nor did he realize there were now more trees around him than automobiles.

The radio station was beginning to fade out, but still there was no need to touch the dial. The static, although it filled the vehicle, did not come within a thousand miles of his consciousness. Only the crowd of mourners, sobbing into soaked handkerchiefs, wondering why the dedicated fall but the unruly continue to stand. The car might as well have been a spaceship on autopilot, traveling through far-off galaxies and constellations. Nobody aboard but one conquered soul, unwilling to return home. As he traveled, some semblance of clarity might have been heard on the radio had someone been listening, but although the static was fading and clarity growing, it continued to go unnoticed.

Maybe I'll leave. I can't stay around here much longer. Everybody looking at me all the time and thinking what a bad thing I did. What a bad son I am. I can't just sit here and listen to this forever.

The vehicle continued down the quiet path, slower than was customary for the nineteen-year-old driver.

As a voice on the radio became louder and clearer, Joseph's awareness was challenged. The thoughts that had so dominated the trip were slowly giving way to an outside influence.

"Man's goal in life should be to surpass his life."

What was this voice intruding on his precious thoughts? Joseph's impulse was to shut the radio off, but something kept him from doing it. Something removed his hand from the dial. The voice continued, "Man should also want this for his family and his loved ones. You see, there is something you must understand, you people out there who consider yourselves Christians on Sunday, but anything but Christians the rest of the week. You need to understand that, to a Christian, death is not to be feared. For a real Christian, death cannot overcome you. Why? Because you've been promised everlasting life. You see a lot of people go to church, and they read the stories about the blood and the lamb and the cross and they think, hey, this sounds like a pretty good deal. And I agree, it does sound pretty good. But the problem is that when the smoke clears, when all eyes are on such a person, and his heart is bearing witness to the world, it becomes apparent that he doesn't really trust that the Lord is at work, not in his life, not in the world, not in his soul. He doesn't really believe it, and *that* is where we get into trouble! You see, God is not a toy God! He's not playing God! So we shouldn't be playing God's people."

Joseph was now caught up in the oration of the unknown speaker. Every word of his voice fell like a missile into Joseph's meditation.

"A man who has God's love, and knows he has God's love, has to fear but one thing. What's that one thing? That one thing is that his children and loved ones may not follow in that wonderful glorious light, even though he is using everything within his being to direct them there.

"Let me tell you a story. There was a young man named Jeremiah. He was about thirty-five, maybe forty years old. He lived down in Tulsa, Oklahoma back in the early 1920s. He went to church every Sunday; took his family to church every Sunday. He was a good man, a loved man, a God-fearing man. Word has it he was a Deacon, but I'm not positive about that. He had two kids, I think they were just nearing their teenage years.

"Anyway, down there in Oklahoma they had a situation where a young brother was caught making a pass at a white woman in an elevator, or something like that, and you know, when some white men got wind of that they wasn't too happy about it. Well, one thing led to another, and the young brother ended up getting hauled off to jail.

"The local newspaper ran a story saying that the woman had actually been assaulted, which wasn't the case, but it did work a lot of people up even more than they already were. Later on, as word started to spread about the story, some of the more intolerant white folks in town got together and decided they were going down to that jail and pay that nigger a little visit. But when they got there, to their surprise, there were already some brothers standing out front with guns.

"And guess who was standing right there with them? You got it, Jeremiah. These brothers figured they ain't going to let them take this brother and string him up without no trial or nothing. You know, that's what they did to brothers who got caught looking at white women in those days. Now this was big time stuff! These white folks didn't like that at all! These brothers standing out front with weapons like they was ready to fight. They was ready to have it out right there on the jailhouse steps, but the police wasn't about to let that happen, so they tried to send everybody home. Well, before the police could get things under control this white man tries to take this brotha's gun. They get to tussling back and forth over the gun and sure enough the white man winds up shot. They say from that very second, the riot was on.

"When Jeremiah got home, he found out that a couple of brothers had been grabbed by an angry mob and were nearly beaten to death. These white folks was getting together by the hundreds and heading toward the black section of town, and they wasn't coming to talk.

"Now this is the part of the story that I want you all to really pay attention to and understand. I was told that when Jeremiah heard what was happening and what was going on, he went over to the corner of the house. You know, back then most black folk wasn't living in no big luxury houses. We didn't have rooms here and rooms there. It was pretty much just one room that everybody did all the cooking, eating, and sleeping in. Well, he went into the corner of the room and he knelt down to pray. His wife was sitting with the kids, and she was crying and carrying on 'cause she knew that Jeremiah was going to get his gun and go out to meet those white folks again. But the kids, they just kind of watched everything, 'cause they didn't really know what was going on."

As Joseph listened to the story he couldn't help comparing this "Jeremiah" the man spoke of, to his own dad. The similarities were clear. The man speaking had succeeded in briefly wrestling Joseph's attention away from his own sorrow."

The voice continued, "Old Jeremiah, he knelt down there and he prayed for about a half-hour. When he arose, he pulled his wife aside and talked to her for awhile, then he gave her a hug and a kiss. He turned around and walked over to his children. When he sat down to talk to those kids he did it so calmly that you would've thought that he was going out for a morning walk afterwards. He told them,

'Make sure you put on clean underclothes for church on Sunday, and don't give your mamma no grief about it. When the reverend asks you to pray, I want you to let God know that you're going to be there praying to him every Sunday of your life, that all you want is to know what he wants you to do with your life. Can you do that for me?' That's all he said. He made sure each of them said yes to what he told them, and then he told them both he loved them and gave them each a hug.

"Then Jeremiah picked up his rifle and walked straight out the door. Just like that. His family never saw him again, never heard what happened to him, never heard a thing. But down there in Tulsa, still to this day, there is an empty grave bearing his name. Today it's estimated that over three-hundred people were killed in the Tulsa race riots of 1921, most of them black, many of them women and children.

"But what makes me wonder, what always makes me rack my brain when I think about that day, is: How could a man have been so calm about everything, under such extreme circumstances? Circumstances obviously beyond his control. Just imagine what must have been going through Jeremiah's mind. What could he have said in those prayers that put his mind at ease during that trying time? I mean, leaving behind his wife and children when he had no idea what was in store for any of them. What do you think? Do you know what I think? I think he was making a deal with God."

As the anonymous voice continued the story, his voice began to revert back and forth from quiet whispers to thunderous shouts.

"I think he knew that he was a man who had the presence of God inside him, so he didn't have to worry what fate was awaiting him outside that door. What he was concerned about were his children! Why was he concerned about his children? Because they didn't know God yet! They needed more time! I think Jeremiah made an agreement with God: 'Hey, fine, if it's my time to go, I'm ready! I just ask that you grant my kids more time to get to know you. Some more time to form a relationship with you, some more time to draw near to you, some more time to learn to love you.'

"I know some of you out there got to be thinking: How do you know what he was saying in those prayers? He could have been saying anything. You want to know how I know this is what happened? I'll tell you how I know! I know it because no man could be at peace in a situation so large, so monstrous, so out of his control, unless he knew that whoever was in control was working on his behalf. How could he have known his children would be safe, or that his wife would be alive to look after them the next day, unless he knew the deal had been struck? Yes, Jeremiah made a deal, and you know what, God kept his end of the bargain, just as he always does. I know God kept his end of the bargain because if he hadn't I wouldn't be standing hear to talk about it. Jeremiah was my granddad and that little boy he pulled aside to speak to was my father."

Now Joseph was pulling the car over to the shoulder. The tears were falling as freely as raindrops, and he knew beyond all doubt that what he was hearing was not by coincidence. He buried his face in his hands, half in amazement at how his personal suffering could be addressed so clearly by a stranger's tongue, and half because so many thoughts, ideas, and revelations were crashing down upon him all at once. The voice continued to direct its message to him as if he were the only listener.

"There are people who feel so close to God, so connected with God, so at peace with him, that their life takes on new meaning. Then, at that point, all that's needed in their lives is to bring their loved ones into that pure relationship with the Almighty. But it can't be done. No matter how hard you try, how hard you press, how much you love, it can't be done. All that you can do is ask God to keep his arms open wide, and to keep giving that person chance after chance to come and be born again.

"See, we can't make somebody give his life to God, and God won't make somebody bow down to him. My granddad knew this all too well. He knew that it had to be a decision his children made for themselves. That's why religious parents are praying all the time. You kids out there think that your parents are praying day and night and ten times on Sundays for themselves, or for a new car, or for help with the bills, but they're not—they're praying for you! That's it. They're praying for you. That's every God-fearing parent's dream—for their child to give their life to the Lord. Any Christian father or mother would gladly—gladly I tell you—lay down their life in the blink of an eye for that gift. So now, let me ask you, has someone been praying for you? Has someone been pleading with God on your behalf? Has someone been praying prayer after prayer and wearing out their knees in hopes that you might one day find your way? I'll bet someone has! Who knows, someone may even have given their life for somebody listening to this message, just in hope that you might find that ultimate love. But whatever they may have done, the fact remains that all your parents, or anybody else can do, is pave the way for you. They can lay the foundation. They can let you know that God loves you. The same way Jeremiah did, they can pray, and they can use their lives to make sure you have every chance and every opportunity to come to the Lord. Then, what's left for you to do, is to give it to Him. I mean give Him everything. All the honor, all the glory, let Him be your guide. Let Him make the decisions. Believe me, He won't steer you wrong. He hasn't made a wrong decision in over two-thousand years, and He won't make one with you, I promise."

Joseph could no longer keep silent. He cried out loud, "I didn't know."

He repeated over and over again, "I didn't know, Daddy, I'm sorry, I didn't know."

It was clear that his life was one of those that this voice on the radio was speaking of. Joseph knew that someone had died for him in order that he may have the opportunity to find life's true meaning. He struggled to compose himself. Each time he reached up to wipe the tears away from his eyes, more fell. They were beginning to sting, and he could feel the redness and the swelling, but still they continued to fall. His shirt was getting damp.

Joseph exited the car, and after struggling to fight back more tears, he opened his eyes, and suddenly became aware of his remote surroundings. There were trees on each side of him. He could smell the pine in the air. The birds were calling praises, and the air was cool

LOW ROAD TO HEAVEN

and fresh. The car door was still open and the speaker's voice could still be heard. It was now joined by a flock of supporters who assisted in a slow, methodical version of "God Has Smiled on Me," complete with piano and organ in the background. As Joseph heard the simple rendition, he half smiled through the tears and the pain.

"God has smiled on me, he has set me free. Whooooh, God has smiled on me, he's been good to me."

Over and over again he heard the words. He began to move his lips along with the choir, although he was careful not to make a sound. The exquisite voices were not to be intruded upon. He then took in a deep breath and surveyed the landscape. After acknowledging the beauty that enclosed him on all sides he walked only a few feet away, off of the paved road into the dirt clearing, faced the setting sun, and knelt down on his knees. There, before the eyes of nature, and no one else, he was swept away. Caught up in a tidal wave of altering passions. The spirit held him closely and he knew first-hand this irreplaceable love he had often heard about but never really been able to grasp. When he arose, his life was no longer his own, but his creator's.

Chapter 9

The New Testament says nothing of apostles who retired and took it easy.
Billy Graham

There was silence in the room. As Joseph stared through the water in his eyes at the minor imperfections in the wood on the boardroom table, he began to unmindfully wipe away at the puddle of tears. Everybody in the room was stunned when Joseph himself broke the silence with words that he apparently couldn't hold back. "It was like I had been sliced right down the center with some kind of flaming sword from heaven—half of me filled with joy and running to my beloved creator, ready to rest in his arms, but still, the other half of me resisted. For years I walked around stuck in this spiritual middle ground. Now I know what John meant when he wrote that "light has come into the world, but men loved darkness rather than light because their deeds were evil."

Joseph's voice was low and beginning to crack. James Quincy quietly left his seat, picked up a box of tissues, and brought them to his friend. Then he put his hand on his shoulder and gave a gentle, but supportive, squeeze. The silence continued for a few more seconds. It was Pastor Wendell who finally decided what needed to be said. "Well, son, we certainly appreciate your talking to us about those things in your life that you obviously hold sacred. I don't believe anybody in this room will ever doubt your devotion to this life you've chosen to lead. Would you like to go to the restroom to kind of get yourself together? If you could return when you're ready, I promise we won't keep you much longer."

Joseph took the reverend up on his idea. In the bathroom he went into the stall and sat on the closed toilet seat. He was glad it was over. He wondered how the board would respond to all they had heard. He had said things to them that he hadn't anticipated saying, but he wasn't sorry. Everything he said was the truth, and if it wasn't acceptable to them, then that's just what he'd have to live with. He washed his face again, and for a moment considered how the prayers he had asked at this particular sink less than an hour ago had been answered in a way that he wouldn't have imagined. Then he returned to the boardroom.

Pastor Wendell didn't wait long before he started speaking. "Well, Joseph, the interview process is over. Normally, we would have you go home and then contact you in a few days to let you know the outcome, but we're not going to do that here. While you were in the restroom we got to talking, and we realized it's pretty unanimous. We want you as our associate pastor here at De Angeles Memorial Church, so if you'll have us, we're offering you the position." Joseph accepted the job, assuring the group that he would do the best he possibly could in his new position.

After all the congratulations and pats on the back, Pastor Wendell quietly excused all the people on the board and invited Joseph to stay for a moment to chat. Joseph wasn't quite sure what to expect. He had heard from his grandfather that Louis Wendell ran a tight ship, so it was possible that warnings and expectations were at hand. The pastor took his seat at the head of the long table and invited Joseph to sit closer. "So, how do you feel about your new duties?"

Joseph responded, "I'm nervous, but I'm excited. I can't wait to get started."

"Well, I'm sure you'll do just fine. I've had you pegged for this position ever since you graduated from seminary. Your grandfather also feels you're ready."

"Yeah, he's been schooling me. He doesn't let me backslide at all. I'm lucky to have him around."

Pastor Wendell then changed the subject to something Joseph hadn't expected. "You know, I already knew a lot of what you told us a little while ago, but I didn't know all of it. I want you to know I really admire your truthfulness about everything you've been through. That kind of truthfulness will certainly pay off in the ministry."

"I'm glad you think so. I plan to do anything and everything I can to spread the Word to the masses."

"There's something else I want you to know. It's that I remember the day when your father left to go visit you at school. You know, he came to visit me at my home. As a matter of fact, he was on his way to the airport when he came by."

Joseph answered in a tone that showed an obvious sense of surprise. "Really? I didn't know that."

"I make it a point to never tell people about my conversations with those who come to me seeking any prayer or counseling, but somehow I don't think your dad would mind me telling you this. It's nothing earth-shattering, really, it's just that I want you to know that he wanted this for you so badly. He wanted you to find the narrow road that's elusive to so many people. I can't tell you how happy I am to have you sitting here before me today, ready to take over pastoral duties in this church that your grandfather started." With a bit of a chuckle he added, "I honestly believe that if anybody ever held God hostage to answer a prayer, it was your dad. We must have prayed together about you for over an hour before he got on that plane."

Joseph just sat and listened. He was moved by the touching reminder of his father's hopes and dreams for his only son.

While driving home that afternoon, Joseph's mind wandered. It wandered back to that day twelve years ago, the day he left for school. It seemed that he didn't even recognize that nineteen-year-old kid, still wet behind the ears. He was in such a hurry to make use of his newfound independence back then. He pondered the reality that those things that brought happiness to him *now* were so different from what brought him happiness back then. He now desired things that he never cared for as a young man. He wondered how his best buddies of that day were doing now. There was no doubt that wherever Buzz was, he was doing all right. Thinking about Jovan, on the other hand, caused him considerable concern.

As his mind drifted near and far, Joseph pulled up to the cemetery. He knew it was where he needed to be. It was time his father knew his son had found his way home, and the Almighty had kept his end of the bargain. He had been here many times over the years to visit his mom. As Joseph surveyed the landscape, memories of sitting and talking with her for hours on end throughout his teenage years swarmed over him like harmless ghosts welcoming him to their sanctuary. Never had he imagined in those days that he would eventually be coming to visit his dad as well.

Being at the cemetery was different since his dad had been buried. There was a discomfort that persisted. No longer was he able to just sit and speak freely as he had always done with his mother. Allan Shaw was buried side-by-side with his wife. Since Dad had arrived, Joseph felt the need to consider his words before he spoke them. In the beginning, it was clearly an issue of pain and of sorrow, sorrow that would no doubt accompany any loving son visiting the gravesite of his parents. But as this common, yet severe, distress began to eventually pass, something else remained. Something remained that refused to relinquish its hold as the years went by.

Joseph walked slowly through the grass, glancing here and there at different markers and flowers. As he drew closer to his revered destination, his head hung low. He looked up barely enough to stay on the correct path. Joseph tugged a bit at his tie as he walked. His suit was now feeling much too stiff, and he couldn't quite relax the way he wanted to. When he finally arrived at the site, he stood silent. All the dialogue he had contemplated on the drive over suddenly took flight. In the quietness of the greenery, the stillness of nature, his mind raced, but nothing came forth. Even the tears that had honored this great man (in the darkness of countless nights) had abandoned the beholden mourner.

Suddenly, the silence was broken. A child's voice could be faintly heard in the distance. Even at long range, Joseph could tell the boy was shouting, merely by the tone in his voice. As Joseph looked around, he caught sight of the youngster who was showing little if any respect to a mother on her knees. The mom pleaded for the toddler to sit and stop his antics, but he only continued. Joseph stood and watched as her rising cries hinted at her mounting anxiety. She had brought flowers for her loved one, but had not yet placed them on the grave, for her attention was so scattered. They appeared to be roses, and were lying far off to her side. Neither she, nor the boy, noticed the lone gentleman in their company, but Joseph could tell she was young. He watched as her auburn hair fluttered about in the breeze, causing her to appear even more frantic as she jerked and stretched about trying to grab the child. Joseph imagined all that had happened in the young boy's life that would change his future forever—even if the child might not understand any of that now.

Joseph witnessed the young mother's utter grief; she appeared so delicate. He mentally leaped from one possibility to the next. He imagined how little this child might have gotten to know his father, and how he couldn't understand what trials and difficulties lay in wait for him and his suffering mother. And what of the father? Now the magnificent struggle of molding a human spirit would have to be left to another. Neither the pride, nor the pain, would ever be his to enjoy.

Joseph gazed back at his dad's headstone. He read the words more slowly than he had ever read them before:

Here lies Allen Henry Shaw, Junior
He was made a little lower than the angels. He lived his life in turmoil because he wanted to be christ-like. Because he lived his life in turmoil, he progressed to be more than he had ever dreamed he could. He was a good father. He was a good husband. He was a good man. He was a good servant. Here lies nothing more than dust and ashes, for it is more certain than the sunrise that Allen Shaw has gone home to become one with his divine creator.

Joseph looked back at the woman and child. They slowly headed toward the parking lot. She held the boy's hand tightly, pulling him along. He fought her every step of the way. Joseph looked back at the resting place where she had knelt. The flowers still sat off to the side, closer to the neighboring grave than to the one she had come to visit. He felt sorrow for the hardships that likely loomed in the future for this woman and her young son.

He looked at his mother's headstone and spoke to her as easily as if she had been standing beside him. "I'm sorry I haven't been here in a while. I've been wanting to come, but I couldn't get out here. But wait until I tell you what I have been doing."

He then turned to his father's grave and took a deep breath. "Dad, I have some good news. I just found out today that I'm gonna be the associate pastor at De Angeles Memorial. Can you believe it? I have to give my first sermon in four weeks." His voice was barely above a whisper. He paused, looking around as if he were expecting help from somewhere on what to say next. "You know, I'm going to have Granddad help me put it together." Silence again.

The shame was with him. He struggled and fought. His voice changed as he mustered the strength to talk. "Dad, I know my needs now. I didn't know them before. I couldn't understand what needs you were always talking about, but I do now. I know 'em now! I needed Him. I always wondered where you got all the...the...the serenity from. Things that got to other people, things that made most folks crazy, never seemed to bother you. I know where you got it now though. I don't quite have it yet myself, but I do know where *you* got it."

Joseph stopped. He walked over to the headstone and placed his hands on the cold, flat surface. After leaving his hands there long enough for the chill to subside and the marble to feel warm under his palms, he began to smile. "I want to thank you, Pop. Just for loving me that much. You didn't know I would find my way, but you gave yourself just to give me the opportunity. Thank you so much."

The sky was clear, and the breeze had a slight chill in it. Joseph breathed in deeply and received the light wind going up into his nostrils. He then whispered as he exhaled. "Thank you, Jesus. Thank you, Jesus." Joseph knew from that moment forward that he and his father would be in perfect harmony. He knew that throughout all time and space he was exactly where he was supposed to be according to divine plan, and his father had been instrumental in getting him there.

That night Joseph celebrated with his family. His grandmother, Crystal, prepared a meal that left not a morsel to be desired. Being the wife of a retired minister, Mrs. Shaw knew how to host a dinner! She was the perfect complement to her husband: a beautiful yet conservative dresser, a spiritual and loving person, and the best cook any of her friends and family had ever known. In the eyes of Crystal Shaw, nothing was too good for her grandson, the newly appointed minister, and it showed when everyone stepped into the dining room.

The sweet potatoes were especially commendable. Since she knew they were a favorite dish of her grandson's, she went the extra mile, adding the marshmallows and brown sugar. This always gave them that special something that moved the partaker of the dish from mere satisfaction to near bliss. Jasmine also helped with the cooking. She was also very skilled in the kitchen, and since she too felt nothing was too good for her brother, she had made numerous desserts. Sweet potato pie, peach cobbler, and banana pudding could all be found on the table. Everybody knew there was more food than could possibly be eaten, but the fact that it was all prepared so beautifully and abundantly made them feel more welcome.

But the truth is, the food was not the main focus of the evening. It wasn't really even out of the norm. Crystal Shaw cooked large dinners for her family regularly, and those present at each dinner always noted it was a notch better than the last. Joseph, one or two of his friends, and Jasmine with her husband and two children, made it a regular date to eat at the home of their grandparents each weekend. Crystal and her husband Allen expected nothing less. And, being sent home with an extra plate of food for tomorrow was always a benefit of dining at the Shaw residence.

But this night was special for another reason: Joseph was following in the footsteps of his grandfather, the celebrated founder of De Angeles Memorial Church. Allen Shaw, Sr. was such a revered person in the local area that he was often quoted in the media and courted by politicians to address community issues. Very few people could be said to match his influence when it came to issues important in the community, and very few people received as many waves and nods when passing through the various neighborhoods of De Angeles.

On this night, Allen Shaw, Sr. took the spotlight off of himself and allowed it to shine on his grandson. He saw the evening as the beginning of a change that, throughout all his hopes and prayers, he had at times feared would never come. He showered his rising saint with praise upon praise.

The meal was started with a prayer that would have been fitting for a full-fledged call to worship at any Sunday service. The honors circled the table, as everyone gave thanks for the new servant who had risen in their midst. The whole house burst with energy and praise. In the middle of dinner, the men and women raised glasses—some filled with wine, others filled with juice—in recognition of Joseph's accomplishments. The excited voices easily drowned out the up-tempo jazz melodies that played throughout the night on the stereo.

Through it all, the night's honoree worked hard to remain humble. When the accolades so filled him that his smile overshadowed his modesty he simply played down his part and placed the credit elsewhere. When they clamored for a token speech, he stated only five words, *"To God be the glory."*

It turned out that this was a night Joseph would not soon forget. It was the first night he would spend with his family when the unwanted would not be present. The shame was absent from dinner this night. Not even for a moment did he consider the possibility of someone reflecting on his wretched mistakes of the past. The shame was no longer perched on his shoulder, whispering torturous lamentations in his ear. The moments never arose, as in the past, when his eyes collided with others and he knew, even if only for an instant, that the rage continued to linger. It was this glimpse of rage that always reminded him that the once abundant love of his family was still chained in the dungeons of their hearts. Whether this was for the rest of his life—or only for tonight—Joseph was free to love and be loved, for the first time in twelve years, and it was wonderful.

Chapter 10

Your gospel-mother is somebody God sends for you. Somebody you travel with in your visions. It's somebody in the church, but he sends them to you an' then they your gospel-mother. They pray with you an' take care of you. It took a long time for me to be converted, but ah got it to stay, haven't ah?

Henrietta Gant, former slave

Reverend Allen Shaw, Sr. took exceptional joy in assisting his grandson in preparing for his first full-fledged sermon, but he was careful not to overstep his need. He wanted to be sure that the spirit of the words spoken on the coming Sunday morning would be the Spirit, not of himself, but of his young successor. The task was not difficult, since there was no doubt in either of the two gentlemen that Joseph was fully capable of presenting a powerful, thought-provoking sermon.

It was the second Sunday of the month, the Sunday when the whole choir was present, and they were in rare form on this day. As the choir lifted the emotions of the congregation and moved them to near ecstasy, Joseph sat next to Pastor Wendell, half enjoying the music and half dwelling on every detail of his sermon.

When the last song had been sung, he felt his stomach churning. He sat upright and took in a huge breath of air. He glanced around at all the familiar faces in the audience and delivered one last silent prayer to God before taking this first step. As he approached the podium, he noticed William Reid among the sea of faces. Mr. Reid had been a best friend to Joseph's dad. Joseph had not seen him in a number of years—certainly not since the new minister had joined the clergy. Seeing this man brought forth a gush of emotions in Joseph, many of which felt alien to him. "What is Mr. Reid doing here?" Joseph had wondered many times whatever had happened to Willie.

Now, all of a sudden, like a bolt of lightning, the preacher found himself standing before a microphone in front of a crowd of over a hundred people with no clue as to what he was doing there. Joseph blinked his eyes a couple of times and looked down at the ground. "Okay, get it together, man, get it together." He thought about the way he was to open the sermon. He thought about maintaining the sureness in his voice that his grandfather told him was so vital. He then opened his mouth and spoke.

"Years back, around the turn of the century, I believe, there was an acrobat who lived in Europe. He would cross the Pacific Ocean to come here to the U.S., and what he would do was tightrope walk across Niagara Falls. Every year, just like clockwork, he would come over. Well, after a while, he figured people were getting tired of the same old thing, so one particular year he decided to liven it up a bit. He decided he would walk across the falls pushing a wheelbarrow full of dirt. Well, he got there, and with the crowd watching, he filled up the wheelbarrow with dirt, turned around, and walked all the way across and then back again. All the people started cheering and waving their arms.

"Then he yelled out to the crowd, 'How many of you folks think I could do that again?'

"Well, the crowd started yelling even louder."

"'Yeah, you can do it again, go ahead, we know you can do it!' So the man took the wheelbarrow right over to the edge of the falls and dumped all the dirt down into the water below.

"Then he turned back to the crowd and made his request. 'Okay, I need one volunteer to ride in the wheelbarrow!'"

There was silence. When some of the laughter and giggling subsided, Joseph asked the congregation, "Are you ever like that? When you hear Jesus prompting you to join him, when you can see the road he's placing before you and it doesn't quite look like what you had in mind, do you get in his wheelbarrow, or do you stay in the crowd and just cheer?" The congregation fell silent.

From behind him, Joseph heard a sincere "amen," which came from none other than Pastor Wendell, and at that precise second the words became like drops of rain during a morning drizzle. He need only mentally reach out, and the words were at his fingertips. What came forth was pure splendor.

As his family sat in the balcony—as a favor so as not to make the young man too nervous—the brilliance that captivated them was so unexpected that for a while it seemed as if they were watching an absolute stranger. The genuine passion for God and for man that Joseph displayed was something none of them had ever glimpsed in him before. He challenged his onlookers to change their lives. He reminded them that their financial gifts and Sunday morning visits were inadequate. He told them, "The only thing you can give God that he doesn't already have is your love and your faithfulness." By the close of the sermon, the congregation was filled with clapping hands and tear-stained faces. Even Joseph himself was moved to the brink of tears as person after person came to the altar to profess a newfound faith. As his grandfather looked on, it seemed to him that this day was no doubt the commencement of a life strewn with triumph and honor.

On this much-anticipated day, Joseph was far beyond what anyone could have expected. His smooth, unhurried speaking style had impressed his grandfather time and time again as he gave informal rehearsals in what used to be his dad's study. But Allen Sr. had assumed that, like most public speakers, the fluidity would diminish in front of a live congregation. The opposite actually occurred.

On the following Monday evening, Joseph dined with Louis Wendell. Joseph was fully aware that on Monday evenings it was customary for the pastor to explore the highs and lows of the previous day's program with those most heavily involved. This evening was dedicated solely to young Mr. Shaw. Although things appeared to have gone extremely well from Joseph's standpoint, he knew Pastor Wendell was a stickler for detail, and so he still did his share of worrying all Sunday evening. The two dined, with Mrs. Wendell sitting between them. Other than an opening "Congratulations on your first sermon, I really enjoyed it" from the lady of the house, there was no mention of the previous day's events during the meal. After the pork chops and side dishes were disposed of, Mrs. Wendell retired to another room, and the two men remained alone at the dinner table.

Now the stage was set for what Joseph was beginning to think might not be as pleasant a conversation as he had hoped. "Well, Mr. Assistant Pastor, how do you feel about yesterday's service?" Joseph took his time answering. Even though he had felt things went better than he had ever dreamed they could, he didn't want to lay all his cards on the table for fear of appearing overconfident.

"I thought it went okay, I guess."

"Okay, you guess? Let me tell you something about myself. I have always been terrified of allowing any minister to give his first sermon in my church. When I was about your age, I was visiting a church with an uncle of mine, and I had the unfortunate pleasure of witnessing a young man give his first sermon. He was a nice enough young brother, and you could tell that he really knew the Word. He knew it maybe as well as I ever will. But that poor young man got up in front of those people and just completely lost all train of thought. He just froze. It was like, you know when you're watching a grade school kid recite his history report up in front of the class, and the kid doesn't want to look up? He just puts his head down to the paper and reads it quickly in the same monotonous voice from start to finish. I don't know whom I felt sorrier for that day: the boy up at the podium, the pastor who sent him up there, or the congregation who had to sit through it."

The elder gentleman stopped to take a slow sip from his refilled glass of Coke. Then he breathed a deep breath of sorrow for the victims of his story. "As afraid as I was of allowing a first timer to speak at De Angeles Memorial, I knew I would be wrong if I didn't at least give you a shot. Besides, I owed at least that much to your family, regardless of what might happen. Now, with all that said, I want you to know that I would have to work like a Hebrew in Egypt to recall ever hearing a better sermon than the one you gave yesterday morning. And I'm talking about *any* sermon, not just a newcomer's."

The zeal with which Joseph gave his "Thank you, sir" made it extremely evident that the grand compliment took him by surprise.

"Now, I don't want you to get too ahead of yourself. I'm sure you've gotten more than enough pats on the back, but you remember, exaltation can bring about one's downfall just as quickly as humiliation. Without putting too much pressure on you, I want you to know that if you can keep your head and heart in the right spirit, you will lead this church to places neither I nor your grandfather ever came close to reaching."

Joseph was stunned. He had expected some compliments might be in order, but Louis Wendell was not a man who regularly handed out praise. The longtime image Joseph had held of a stern captain at the head of his ship, quick to send dissidents off the plank at the slightest hint of contention, was beginning to give way. Joseph began to see his pastor as more of a brilliant oddity, overjoyed to discover a fellow virtuoso, and eager to groom him for glory. What once intimidated Joseph about this man seated before him now clearly astonished him. Not many men of status are capable of seeing great proficiency in an associate without feeling threatened. The ease and comfort with which the tributes fell from his lips impressed Joseph even more than the actual remarks themselves.

It was now official: Joseph was not only an associate pastor at a prominent church; according to Pastor Wendell he was the future of De Angeles Memorial. The next few months only worked to confirm what Pastor Wendell already suspected, that his young assistant was indeed genuinely gifted. Joseph worked harder and harder on every sermon, in a constant effort to maintain the high ideals set for him by his mentors. The result was a steady rise to prominence for the young minister. The word began to spread throughout the city of a rising star in the service of God. Requests began coming in for Joseph to be a guest speaker at neighboring sanctuaries. The Shaw family doted on their young sensation. Joseph's grandfather stayed in his grandson's ear with words of wisdom, and instructed the boy on how best to remain humble. Joseph listened, and the more success seemed to give chase, the more humble he was determined to remain. And through it all, his relationship with Louis Wendell flourished.

It took some time, but the new position helped Joseph at long last to begin to get used to the idea of living alone in what he had known as "his father's" house. Jasmine visited regularly with the kids, which helped a lot. She and her brother had seemed to grow closer since he had become a minister. Joseph felt that she now, for the first time, began to look at him as a serious adult.

Chapter 11

It amazes me how we learn to call a rainstorm "bad."
There's nothing more beautiful than a storm.
Leonard Peltier

On a particular Friday evening after finishing dinner, Joseph chatted away on the telephone with his close friend, James Quincy. The two casually joked about this and that. As he talked, laughed, and flipped the channels on the television, all at once there was a barely detectable knock on the door. Joseph was curious, since he had made no plans for company. As he sauntered toward the door, he continued his conversation on the telephone. He expected to find either Jasmine or his grandfather waiting on the other side of the doorway.

Not bothering to ask who it was, Joseph opened the door. For a moment he was taken aback. The person visiting was not his sister or grandfather, but a woman whom he did not recognize. Rushed hellos were exchanged, but then there were a few seconds of silence. Joseph then noticed that James was still on the line chatting away. "Um, say, brother, can I call you back in a moment? Okay, thanks." Joseph then regained his composure and asked, "How can I help you?"

The woman was attractive. She was wearing a jeans outfit that looked rather new, and her hair was dyed an obvious blonde. For some reason she appeared to be nervous. She looked at him and looked away, looked at him and looked away. The woman finally said, "Joseph Shaw, I can't believe I'm here." Her voice took Joseph by surprise. It was familiar, very familiar. He stared at her.

He meant to think to himself, but the words came out, in a low, choppy whisper, "Where do I know you from?" but suddenly, in mid-sentence, his mind jolted into place. "Sharonda. Oh, my God, I mean oh my...what are you doing here?"

Sharonda smiled as if she were relieved. "I knew you would recognize me. I hope you don't mind me surprising you like this. I got your address from your friend, Buzz. If you want me to leave, I can come back some other time."

"No, I wasn't really doing anything, but wow! I can't believe it's you. How long has it been—like ten years?"

Sharonda casually replied, "Closer to twelve, actually."

Joseph invited her in, but she didn't sit down. The two made a little awkward small talk. Although it crossed both of their minds already more than once, neither dared approach the subject of what had transpired between the now-imprisoned Paris Downey and Joseph. He continued to stare at her in astonishment. "Sharonda Atkins, I still can't believe it's you."

Sharonda returned a half smile and shyly cocked her head to the side as she teased Joseph. "So this is De Angeles, huh? I see why you like it here so much. It's got that quiet "little house on the prairie" feel to it. If I had looked down to change the CD, I would have passed it up."

Joseph laughed as he replied. "Little house on the prairie? Now here you go. You know it ain't all that. We ain't quite milking cows and raising chickens yet."

They continued to talk, and when she found out that her former boyfriend was now a minister, she was overjoyed. She told him she had always known that he would eventually amount to something, and that their time together had been one of the better decisions in her life. When Joseph asked about Sharonda's life since the two had last talked, she lost the edge of excitement in her voice.

"Things haven't been real easy for me the last few years. That's why I'm here."

Joseph showed concern in support of his guest. "Hey, if there's any way I can be of help, just say the word, I mean it." Sharonda paused for a moment, and then told Joseph she'd be right back. As she walked out the front door, Joseph went to the window. He was curious as to what could be so important to warrant her leaving in the middle of such a significant conversation. After she disappeared into the parking lot, Joseph was forced to sit on the couch and wait. As he sat, he reminisced, and was smothered in both delightful reflections and horror-stricken ghosts, all conjured up by the mere presence of this woman. Some of the best and worst times he could recall living through were tied to the few months they had spent together. He honestly had no clue as to how he should feel about her, or why she would suddenly show up at his door thousands of miles away after so many years.

At last, the knock on the door came. There were questions and statements already on Joseph's mind as a result of his few moments of contemplation, but as he opened the door they went away as quickly as they had arrived. Sharonda was accompanied by a young boy. The boy was dressed in a T-shirt and shorts, although the weather warranted much more. He had on a gray baseball cap turned slightly, but strategically, to the left. His eyes were in a fixed stare, as if something unusually interesting were on the ground in front of him. After a mild look of surprise, Joseph said hello to the young man, but the boy didn't respond. Sharonda introduced the boy to Joseph as Alfonzo. She then told Joseph that Alfonzo was her twelve-year-old son. A silence took over the trio for more than a couple of seconds. Joseph then asked in an anxious voice, "Is there something you're trying to tell me here?" Sharonda didn't respond. He then suggested, in the most forceful tone anyone had used all evening, "Come into my room for a minute so we can talk." They quickly excused themselves from young Alfonzo as she followed Joseph into a back room.

"Sharonda, if you have something you need to say to me, you need to say it right now!"

Sharonda responded in an equally forceful tone, "He's yours, okay, that's what I came here to tell you. He's your son!"

Joseph shook his head and turned away. "I can't believe this! Twelve years later! Twelve years later you come to me with this! What am I supposed to do with this? You bring me this grown kid whom I don't even know—I never even knew existed—and say I'm his father? How am I supposed to believe you? I'm a minister now! Do you know how this is gonna look for me?"

Sharonda answered, now in a more somber voice. "Look, I didn't come here to ruin your life. I never meant for it to come to this. I didn't know what to do. I didn't think you would ever want anything else to do with me after what Paris did to your father. I knew you wanted to leave after all that, and I didn't want to try and make you stay.

"Yeah, I wanted to leave! But that's got nothing to do with you keeping this from me all these years!"

"Well, what then? What would you have done if I had told you, 'Hey, Joseph, I know my boyfriend just shot your father but I'm pregnant, and you're the daddy, so we got other stuff to deal with?' What would you have said then?"

"I don't know. I would have said something! I wouldn't have just disappeared for twelve years!"

"Joseph, I knew I couldn't tell you at that time because things were so crazy with what had happened. I figured I would wait a little while and then tell you, but I don't know what happened. The days started turning into months, and the months turned into years, and before you know it, here I am. I'm sorry."

"Well, sorry ain't gonna cut. Does this boy know who I am? Does he know anything about me?"

"I had always told him his dad was in California. The other day I told him that it was time I brought him to meet you."

"And here you are. Does he know that I had no idea about him, or does he think I just ran away?"

"I told him you didn't know."

As Sharonda spoke, Joseph stood facing the wall with one hand flat against the eggshell-colored paint, and the other on his hip. His eyes were shut tightly as he continued to shake his head in disgrace.

"Joseph, you have to understand. I thought I could do it on my own. I don't mind if you hate me for what I did, but please don't take it out on Alfonzo. It's not his fault. He's your son. I know he's your son because after Paris got sent to prison they gave him a blood test to establish paternity. They said he wasn't the father, and I was glad he wasn't the father. Alfonzo's blood type is A-positive, and your blood type is A-positive, isn't it? I know it is, because mine isn't, and he has to have either my blood type or yours. He's your son, and, to be honest with you, I was glad when I realized he was yours. That meant he had some good genes, your genes, not that murdering no-damn-good-for-nothing's genes. There was nobody else, just you and Paris."

Joseph glanced out at the boy to make sure he couldn't hear the bitter conversation taking place. "So why now? Why show up now if you didn't feel the need to fill me in for twelve years?"

Sharonda was now straining to talk through the tears. "All the men in my life ain't shit. I don't want him to grow up to be a nobody. I want him to grow up to be somebody good and decent and smart like you. I caught him smoking some weed last month. He cuts school all the time. I didn't know what else to do. He's smart, and he treats people real good and kind, just like you always did. I'm so glad he got your personality. He just learns all the wrong stuff. You know where I live. He just can't grow up the right way on them streets."

The distress remained deeply imbedded on Joseph's face. He kept his eyes shut tightly and spoke out loud to nobody in particular, "I can't believe this is happening! I can't believe this! What am I supposed to do with this?"

Even though he didn't talk to her directly, Sharonda, hoping to add some helpful suggestions, and maybe appeal to Joseph as a member of the clergy, suggested: "You can teach him all about God and Jesus and all that stuff. That's what he needs, something to believe in." Joseph appeared to pay her no mind as he continued thinking out loud.

Joseph felt his life slowly slipping away. He considered his grandfather, Allen Shaw, Sr., and all the lofty dreams that had been conjured up in recent months. He thought about the unexpected words of Pastor Louis Wendell the day after his first sermon, "You will lead this church to places neither I nor your grandfather even came close to reaching."

Both anger and fear enveloped him. "How can I tell this to the family? I'm going to be a failure again, just like before!" His eyes began to fill with tears. He again faced the wall, this time purposely to hide his sorrow. Joseph tried hard to regain his composure so he might apologize for his melodramatic behavior. When he got as much control as he possibly could, he suggested that Sharonda and the young man sleep in the guest room for the night, and that they could further discuss the situation in the morning, to which she agreed.

The night was long and restless. Should he call a friend to get advice, or should he try to do something to get his mind away from this for the night? With his eyes half-closed, he stared at the ceiling. All the minor details of his room seemed more noticeable than usual—the one-inch crack at the base of the window, the peeling paint on the far wall. He conversed with God as slumber finally approached.

But even in rest, the quandaries plagued him. Joseph found himself in a huge field with numerous crops bursting forth—apples and oranges, corn and tomatoes, all ripe for the picking. But he had no time to eat. While all the joyous people around him were reaping the benefits of their harvest, Joseph had allowed himself to be left out in the cold. He rushed to turn his soil and get his crop planted, but he feared he might be too late. As he hastened to make up for his apparent slothfulness, the only one paying any attention to the desperate farmer was a young man unusually attired in a dark suit.

As Joseph labored, the young man walked up slowly, and kindly asked, "Aren't you the preacher?"

"Yes, I am the preacher."

"Well, why don't you preach, then? They are all waiting for you to come and preach."

Joseph replied, "But I haven't cultivated my land yet, don't you see? I'm way behind!"

The man started pulling Joseph away. "Come on, everybody's waiting." Joseph tried to pull away, but the young man was strong. As he struggled, he saw other people come over who began planting their own crops in his section. Joseph kicked and yelled, but he could not break the grip of his tormentor.

Chapter 12

"The Pauper has to die before the Prince can be born."
Meister Eckhart

In the morning it was all rather sketchy in Joseph's mind. He woke up early and started making some breakfast. It was about time to call Jasmine and get some sane input on all of this. As he spoke timidly to his sister in an effort to brace her for the mallet he was soon to drop on her, young Alfonzo walked into the kitchen in his shirt and sweatpants, still with barely-open morning eyes. While still on the phone, Joseph turned to the young man and greeted him, "Good morning, you want some breakfast?"

Without making any eye contact the boy responded, "Yes, please."

"Where's your mother? Still in bed? You'd better go and get her up if she wants to eat this morning."

Joseph continued his conversation with Jasmine. Hardly above a whisper, the boy responded, "She's not here, sir."

Joseph quickly turned directly toward the boy, asking the reflexive question: "What did you say? She's not here? What do you mean she's not here?"

"She left last night."

"Well, where did she go?"

"I don't know. She just woke me up and said she would be back later."

"Be back later! What is she..."

Joseph stopped himself from blowing up at the child. He then took a second to calm himself and to tell Jasmine that he would call back shortly. Next, he sat young Alfonzo down and continued his line of questioning. "So you're telling me your mother gathered her things together last night, woke you up, and told you she would be back later?"

"Yeah, that's what she said."

"Well, by *later* did she mean later today, or later next week, or what?"

"I'm not sure. I didn't get a chance to ask. I think she might have meant later next week. That's what she usually means."

After hearing this last statement, Joseph knew that the situation was serious. As he and the youngster sat together, Joseph managed to get the boy to talk about his upbringing, and about his relationship with his mom. Joseph soon realized that Sharonda had not actually played the central role in raising her son. Alfonzo had spent the majority of his life in the care of his grandmother, June Atkins. His mom came around only on infrequent weekends. That was until Mrs. Atkins came down with some type of illness that forced her into a home for the elderly that offered constant medical supervision. When it seemed Grandma would no longer be available as the caregiver, Alfonzo was back with Mom, moving from place to place. Sharonda's various boyfriends routinely attempted to play part-time dad to her son, some doing the job better than others, but none staying around for more than six or seven months.

As Joseph listened to the boy's story, he thought to himself how things should and could have been different for the young man. Alfonzo was keenly aware of his mom's poor decision-making habits, but it made no difference. He loved her, and he was certain that, regardless of their dire circumstances, she loved him.

Joseph did not call Jasmine back. He and Alfonzo both showered and got cleaned up. After getting dressed, he realized the boy had no clean clothes. He had put back on the same T-shirt that he had arrived in. They got in the car and headed toward Jasmine's house, stopping at the mall on the way to pick up a couple of things.

When they arrived at Jasmine and her husband, Mark's home, his older sister already had a good idea of what was going on. She had her two young sons come and show Alfonzo to their room to entertain him, then she sat down with her brother for the story of what had transpired in the last twenty-four hours. Mark also sat quietly with the two, as he had become a trusted part of the family, and a friend to Joseph over the years.

Joseph told them about how close he and Sharonda had been years ago, and that she had actually been his first real love. They knew that this was the woman whose boyfriend had taken a gun and fired a hole through each of their hearts on a dark summer night long ago. She made it clear that she was making an effort not to hold the blood of her father over the head of this woman, but still, Jasmine was quick to display her contempt for the abandoning mother. Through the whole afternoon, the only real decision that was reached by the three was that as soon as Sharonda returned, legal means would be pursued to bring about the truth concerning Joseph's relationship with the boy. It was difficult, but with the aid of his sister and brother-in-law, Joseph was able to maintain at least the appearance of a positive attitude throughout the day. He tried hard not to show the panic that filled his mind. As he sat and talked, his voice remained even-keeled, and his eyes somber. But inside, his thoughts caused him pain so deep that, had he not been thinking them, he would have hardly been aware that he was capable of feeling to such a tremendous depth. But even so, he knew what he had to do.

He must face the two men most overjoyed by his overwhelming success as a member of the clergy. It was at that point when the wide-reaching implications of these circumstances would fully present themselves.

When his grandfather, Allen, Sr., was told of what had transpired, he was crushed, but he refused to let it show. He knew that his grandson's life must follow the course laid before it, whatever that course entailed. He stood before Joseph and asked the difficult question: "Do you believe this boy is your son?"

When Joseph replied with a quiet, "I don't know," his grandfather only repeated the question with more vigor than previously. Finally, Joseph acknowledged that he did indeed believe Alfonzo to be his.

His grandfather suggested to him that it was then his duty, as a God-fearing man, "to treat the boy as such."

Allen Shaw, Sr. understood that for her to leave her child on the spur of the moment, with a man she hadn't seen in over ten years, implied that Sharonda was not much of a mother to begin with. The child didn't appear to have any family who could be contacted to shed some light on the obscure state of affairs. Mr. Shaw further believed it would be a heinous mistake to suggest any doubt as to the paternity of the boy until more could be learned about his mother. Then he confirmed his grandson's worst suspicion: These new developments could very likely jeopardize Joseph's current standing as associate pastor at De Angeles Memorial Church. But Allen Shaw was not the man to make that decision. He and Joseph both knew who was.

The sooner he sat down with Pastor Wendell, and at least made an attempt to plead his case, the better. So that night he made an unannounced visit to the man he held in so much esteem, to bring his predicament to light. Although it was unexpected, Mr. Wendell appeared happy to see his young protégé on this Saturday evening. The two sat down in the front living room, where it was obvious that the minister had been studying the Word. When Joseph finally found the courage to break the news to his mentor, he expected nothing less than a sound verbal flogging in return. As he made a firm attempt to sit up straight and look directly in the eyes of his superior, he could feel himself wincing in anticipation. As the pastor glared into Joseph's mind, his silence seemed to speak volumes of disappointment. Joseph couldn't move. He was immobilized, not with fear, but with unworthiness. Finally, at long last, the pastor spoke.

"So you feel that you've got a problem, do you?"

"It certainly looks that way, sir."

"Well, I believe that's all in the way you perceive the situation. Are you looking at this from God's perspective or your own?"

What followed was an impromptu in-depth lesson on life from teacher to student. "If you are concerned about this affecting your position at the church, I can understand why you would consider it a problem. The Deacon Board and I will have to have a discussion followed by a vote regarding whether you will be able to remain with us in your current capacity. But, in all honesty, it's not likely you will be able to continue. I'm sorry I have to tell you that so bluntly, but you may as well know what to expect. If you are looking at this situation as to how it will appear to people you know and people around town, I can also understand why you would see this as a problem. People are very fickle by nature. We are quick to judge, and slow to forgive and understand. But what you've got to realize is, these issues are not God's issues. God is not concerned with job titles, nor is He concerned with the word around town. When we first considered you for the position, on that last day of the interview, I told you that we wanted to find out if you were the kind of man whose life was guided by the hand of the Almighty—if you were a man who could display that trust in God when the storm was on its way. Your storm has arrived. It appears to me that the hand of God has selected another path for you. It disappoints me, because I have felt for a while now that I had found one heck of an associate pastor, but you've got to play the hand you're dealt. We don't choose our paths; they're chosen for us."

The Pastor could still see very clearly the pain and disappointment on Joseph's face, and he addressed it. "I know you're upset. It's difficult to have a dream and to see it shattered in the blink of an eye. I've known you for a long time. I remember the look on your face at the funeral when your mom died. You had to be about ten or eleven years old then. Just a little younger than this boy, Alfonzo, I guess."

Joseph wondered where this revisiting of such deep wounds could be leading. He abruptly replied. "I was nine."

The Pastor cautiously continued. "My heart just broke that day as

I thought about how difficult a road lay before you and your family without a mother's love to anchor you. There is no hurt deeper than the hurt of a motherless child. That is why this young boy needs you to accept the road that lies before you with all the zeal you can muster. He's been raised by a grandmother who is apparently all but gone from him now. His mother seems to have always been a very distant entity in his life. And there has been no father. This is a motherless child, and he has been placed on your road. Looking back to that day of your mother's funeral, the only thing I could've imagined worse than losing your mother's love would have been never having that love to begin with. So, when you say you've got a problem, I would have to agree with you. But your problem is not losing your chosen profession—that can be dealt with. Your problem is how to teach a young boy to love and be loved."

Joseph sat quietly. He knew that what had just been dropped in his lap was none other than pure and simple truth. But truth or not he was not happy with the implications. As he sat and listened to the Pastor speaking, Joseph could feel his disappointment turning to frustration turning to anger. He could feel the hostility taking hold of him.

How could they remove me from my position? It's not like I can't preach just because I have a son! I am the best associate pastor this church has ever had! I've had invitations to speak all over this city! After all my family has done for this church this is how they repay me!

When Pastor Wendell was finished speaking, Joseph was still silent, not even willing to look his pastor in the eye. He maintained a look of indifference. He wanted to get out of the house as quickly as possible. "Well I better get going. I don't want to keep *my son* waiting. You know, being a single parent and all."

After noticing a mild look of surprise on Pastor Wendell's face, Joseph felt somewhat guilty for his sarcasm, but he refused to apologize. Instead he stood up and swiftly headed for the door. As he walked through the front room the Pastor's wife caught site of him and innocently offered a sincere "goodbye" to which Joseph responded with a half-hearted wave and a slamming of the front door.

By the time he got to the car Joseph was enraged. He slammed the door shut, then slammed his fist onto the dashboard.

"Damn it! This ain't fair!"

When he turned on the car there was a CD playing of last Sunday's service at DeAngeles Memorial. Joseph ripped the cd from the deck, threw it into the back seat and sped off.

Chapter 13

The evil that men do lives after them.
Henry David Thoreau

"What can I get for you, sugar?"

"Just a cup of hot chocolate and one of those Danishes, please."

"You look beat, child. If you're planning on getting back on the road you might want to have something with a little more kick to it—a cup of coffee or something?"

"No thank you. Hot chocolate will be fine."

"All right then, suit yourself."

Sharonda had been driving for hours with almost no rest. Her eyes were bloodshot, and she knew she would have to be back at work within a couple hours of arriving home. Her stomach was growling, but since payday was still a few days off, a Danish and hot chocolate would have to do. She still had to put gas in the tank before getting back on the highway. She wanted desperately to call her manager and tell her that she wouldn't be in to work this morning, but the thought of hearing that high-pitched, complaining voice was too much to bear. At this time of the morning she was too exhausted to even come up with a decent excuse.

At 3:00 in the morning the coffee shop was nearly empty. Only one other table was occupied. Two young couples sat four booths away, still out from a night of partying. They spoke loudly and laughed often. As she watched them, Sharonda thought about Alfonzo.

In a few years her son would be going out on his first date. Girls would be calling to speak to him and would be writing love notes telling him that he's cute. Her mind went back to the third grade when she wrote her first love note. It was to Darren Miller, a fourth grader. He was the class clown. She remembered the pain she felt when she realized that he had shown the note to all of his friends and within a few short minutes it seemed that the whole school had seen the note. The disappointment was still so vivid in her mind that now, years later, she wondered what could she have seen in Darren Miller that was so attractive. For a class clown, he wasn't even that funny.

In her heart, Sharonda was certain that the young lady Alfonzo eventually would fall for would be a lucky one. He had always been very kind to young women, and never appeared to have had a violent temper.

As she heard the raucous talk a few booths away, a strange uneasiness came over her—a feeling she had certainly felt before, but one that she couldn't quite put a name to. A few days ago, Sharonda had seen her mom lying in a hospital bed, and she had nearly broken down from the shock. June Atkins had been admitted to the hospital nearly ten days ago after a major stroke. When Sharonda showed up to see her mom (already two days into her hospital stay), Mrs. Atkins didn't appear to recognize her only child. She stood and presented herself to her mother again, and again.

"Mom, it's me, Sharonda. It's your daughter. You know, Sharonda Atkins, Mom. Your sugar plum, remember?"

Crying had always been a sign of weakness to her, but she couldn't fight back the tears, no matter how hard she tried. As she held her mom's hand, and spoke words of reassurance, Mom gave only a distant nod and stared back directly through her.

The thought of going back to the hospital was petrifying.

"What if she's doing worse? What then? I can't do it. She didn't even know who I was!"

But Sharonda knew she had to go. She tried to think of a friend who might go with her, but Jahlan, the only friend who would likely offer any comfort, was away visiting family.

"Maybe I should call Dad. I wonder if he knows yet. I bet she would recognize him! She would probably jump out of bed and do the electric slide for him if he walked into the room. I don't even know if I could find his phone number. I'll bet he wouldn't even care. He'd probably send a stupid card or call a month after she's dead like he does for my birthdays."

Although she complained in her head, deep down Sharonda knew that she would make the call. Somewhere, beneath the vast sea of hatred, there was still a longing to connect with him. Although it had been crushed to bits long ago, pieces of a magnificent father-daughter relationship still rested on the floor of her broken spirit, waiting, hoping to someday be reassembled. She never spoke of it. She never acknowledged it even existed. But deep down, in utter darkness, her secret dream remained—shackled, quiet, starving.

In an instant Sharonda had to move her foot. The two couples were leaving, and one young lady partially stepped on her toe with no apology or even a kind smile to follow. Sharonda glared over her shoulder at the girl then shook her head.

"You done ordered this hot chocolate, and now you let it sit here and turn into cold chocolate. You ain't even tasted the stuff, baby. You want me to bring you something else or you want me to freshen that up for you? You get the royal treatment here tonight seeing that you the only one in here and all."

Sharonda smiled back toward the waitress. She was stunned to realize how tall the woman was. How could she not have noticed that before? She had soft brown eyes that reminded her of her mom.

"I'm sorry, could you please just freshen it up for me. I promise I'll drink it this time."

The waitress sauntered off, and Sharonda forgot about her irritation over the incident with her toe.

Sharonda's mind went back to her dad. "His phone number should be in my old phonebook, assuming he hasn't changed it yet. I'll call him tomorrow."

The waitress placed a new cup of steaming hot chocolate in front of her with a mountain of whipped cream on top. Then she sat down and nonchalantly asked, "So what's happening, girlfriend? What is it that's got you in here in the middle of the night drowning your sorrows in hot chocolate, huh?"

Sharonda looked down for a moment, stalling for time. She didn't often discuss her personal business, even with her friends, let alone a strange waitress in a coffee shop. She had always done better sharing her hidden feelings with family pets and stuffed animals. People were never easy to trust. They never really seemed to care. Usually they just asked how she was because they didn't know what else to say. But something about Princess—the name written on the badge—was genuine.

Sharonda thought to herself, *It's 3:00 o'clock in the morning, and I'm over a hundred miles from home; I may as well humor this woman. She has nothing better to do.* "I'm just worried about my son. I just left him with his dad for the first time, and I don't know if he's up to it, ya know."

"Girl, please, the man ain't deranged is he?"

"No, he's a minister."

"A minister! What you talking about, if he's up to it? Ain't nobody more up to it than a minister! Teach that boy about the Lord, I tell you! Most boys growing up today, they don't know nothing about God. You better leave that boy with his daddy for a while. How old is he?"

"He's twelve."

"Twelve years old! He needs his daddy anyway. It's too many women running around here nowadays trying to be the momma and the daddy. You can't do that stuff! Little boys need they daddies. Teach 'em how to be a man. That's why there are so many men out there today all confused not knowin' up from down, nor right from left!"

The sureness in the waitress's words was comforting to Sharonda, even though they were only based on the half-truths she offered.

"Maybe you're right. Maybe I'm just being selfish."

102

"Well, that's all right, sugar. That's what we mothers are supposed to do. If *we* don't watch out for our babies, who will? We just got to know when to let them grow up and spread their wings a little bit, that's all. Call him every now and then. Drop him a letter. I promise you: The world ain't gonna stop turning if you leave that boy with his daddy for a couple of weeks."

Sharonda felt her stomach stiffening. She picked up the Danish and took her first bite. The words *a couple weeks* that the waitress spoke just seemed to hang in mid-air, mocking her. She didn't know when or if she would see Alfonzo again, but a *couple weeks* was never part of the plan. She knew that Princess's version of what we mothers are supposed to do didn't apply to her. Sharonda didn't know who would be watching out for her baby. She had no plans to write. Nor did she bother to ask the phone number to Joseph's house.

"Maybe God will watch out for them if we don't? Doesn't He have a role to play in all of this?"

"God—of course He has a role! But, sweetheart, his role ain't to raise the babies. He just does the hiring and firing for the position. See, like he hired me to watch out for mine, and he hired you to watch out for yours. God knows who is the right person for the job. Even when *we* don't know, He knows.

Sharonda looked at her watch. The lecture on mother-son relationships was not what she had ordered, and she no longer had any inclination to humor this waitress. But before she got up to leave, she figured she would hand this woman a bit of information that flew in the face of her philosophical reasoning.

"I don't think He knew the right person for the job when he gave me my mother. She was the most timid woman you would ever see. She let her husband beat on her, and she loved him anyway. He should have definitely fired her a long time ago."

"You poor baby. That must have broken your heart, going through that."

"I got past it."

"Well, I'll tell you, just because someone is the right person for the job don't mean they perfect and they know all the answers."

"It don't! Well, what the hell makes them the right person then? Anybody can have the wrong answers!"

Princess knew clearly by now that the conversation had taken a path Sharonda would have preferred not to travel. She felt sorry for Sharonda. To Princess, Sharonda represented millions of women around the world, all fed up with going it alone, but the waitress pressed on.

"Sweetheart, listen to me."

Sharonda sighed, and rolled her eyes.

"Please, just listen to what I'm saying. It's what's inside of you that makes you the right person; no, the right *woman* for the job. Come on, you got your own baby now; you've got to feel it sometimes. We all do. It's the love, sugar. It's that thing that eats at you at the thought of leaving your baby for a few days, that feeling when you can't seem to think about nothing else but when will they be back from wherever they might be gone off to. That sigh of relief when they walk in the door and you know your child is safe and sound. That's what makes us the right women for the job—the love. I'll tell you, a child can do a million different kinds of wrong, but sugar, you better know that his mother is gonna love him come Hell or high water. It ain't about knowing all the answers. You asked if God has a role in this. Well, that's His role, knowing all the answers, but you and me? We just gotta love our babies to death and do the best we can with the rest."

Sharonda couldn't ignore what she was hearing, nor could she accept it. Her resentment was deeply imbedded, and refused to be uprooted during this early morning confrontation.

"Well, how is doing the best she can letting some man beat on her? How does that make any sense? She should have been gone the first time he even raised his hand! She should have put his ass in jail!"

"All right, I'm not gonna sit here and say you're wrong; you're probably right. I sure enough would have taken a frying pan to his head if it was me, but it wasn't me, and it wasn't you either. You don't know what was going through your mother's head at that time. He wasn't just *some* man, he was your father. Did you ever think that maybe she didn't leave him because of you?"

"What do you mean because of me? I would have been fine with it if she left."

"I mean that maybe she didn't want to raise her baby girl without a father so she did what she felt she had to do to keep him. See, that's what I mean by a mother's love for her child—what you feel you need to do to put your baby first. Sometimes it's right, and sometimes it's wrong, but you put your child first."

"Well, a lot of good it did her. He left when I was seven."

"And when he left, who raised you then? Who paid the bills then? Who made sure you had food to eat and clothes on your back? When things didn't work out the way she planned, she still did what she had to do to raise her child. And don't think she didn't sacrifice through it all. You got your own baby now, so you know about sacrifice."

Sharonda could take no more. This graveyard-shift waitress had veered off the congenial path and was now carelessly trampling through her delicate conscience. Just as she had feared, it was a mistake to open her emotional lockbox to examination by another human being. The conversation seemed to have taken on an accusatory tone that would never have been present in her confessions to Sherlock, her purple-and black-striped teddy bear.

"I gotta go. I have to work in the morning, and I still have a long drive to get home."

As Sharonda scooted out of the booth, Princess sensed that she had struck more than a chord in the young woman.

"Baby, I'm sorry if what I said bothered you. Sometimes I just run my mouth and won't stop. Things are gonna be fine, you'll see. When you get your son home he's gonna be just as precious as when you left him."

With that, Sharonda flipped a five-dollar bill on the table.

"Keep the change!"

She then turned and hurriedly exited the restaurant. When she got to the car she sat still for a moment. Her contempt for the waitress was bubbling over. She considered the woman's words to be meaningless chatter spoken by someone bored with her job. As she sat there in the car she could feel the same uneasiness still lingering, still clearly present, but more pronounced. She thought about Alfonzo. She envisioned his face when she woke him up to tell him she was leaving for a while. He looked like he suspected it would be more than a while. "I wonder if he's sleeping right now." She thought about her mom lying in a hospital bed. "Is anybody going by to see her? Is anybody taking care of the house? I'm not sure what I'm supposed to do. Why do I have to be the one to take care of this and take care of that? I take care of myself, that's what I can do."

Sharonda started the car, turned on the radio, and headed off toward home. As she drove, the music soon lost its ability to occupy her attention, and only her incriminating thoughts remained. Before long, the uneasiness that had rested in her bosom blossomed into a bright clarity in her mind: The guilt she felt was not to be ignored.

Chapter 14

I wish I had a million dollars, and I could fly away to heaven on silver
wings.
I wish I could always laugh and holler, oh, what a wonderful thing that
would be.
I wish I could get all A's and B's without ever having to worry or slave,
and maybe I'd have a black stallion that always loved to play.
All these things I wish for and sometimes even more,
but when I was just four all I wanted was love and a box of eighty-four
crayons.
Crystal Bolds-Loché (age thirteen)

For the next couple of weeks, each day was filled with a bit more
frustration than the last. For Alfonzo, each morning his hope for the
only piece of mothering he knew—regardless of its deficiencies—was
dashed as he awoke to another lonely sunrise. Sharonda had not
returned, and although these circumstances were all too familiar to
the youngster, for some reason this time his chances for another
interim reunion seemed bleaker than in the past. The depression that
resulted from Sharonda's absence caused much interference in what
Joseph had hoped would be a blossoming father-son relationship. The
more Joseph attempted to invite and encourage Alfonzo's true
feelings and identity, the more the youth pulled away and shut down.

The only time he even momentarily witnessed the boy opening up was when Joseph played bystander to conversations between Alfonzo and his newly-discovered cousins, Mark Jr. and Eric, during one of his frequent visits to Jasmine's house.

Alfonzo was not much attuned to his father's being a preacher. He hadn't been to church very often and didn't care to begin any time in the near future. Even though he communicated with his dad almost exclusively in one-word sentences, Alfonzo never challenged or showed disrespect to Joseph. He chose mainly to tolerate the circumstances while he had to. Most days were spent either in front of the television or listening to music on his Discman headphones, which were the only property he had brought with him on that first night. When he did speak in whole sentences, it was usually to inform his so-called father of how out of touch he was with youth of the twenty-first century. Joseph read books and solicited information wherever he could concerning parenthood, but nothing he tried seemed to help break down that barrier. With each failed attempt at a connection, there appeared another small scratch on his center, that place he once believed could not be punctured with the lengthiest of blades. It was all taking its toll. His patience, his dedication, and even his faith were being battered, like the entrance of a great fortress crumbling under the continuous assault of attacking warriors.

Further inflaming his grief were the reactions Joseph was receiving from various church members, who openly displayed their disapproval of the former pastor's state of affairs. But James Quincy was not one of those people. He was determined to stand by his friend through these difficult times. It was he who kept his buddy informed on what was filtering though the rumor mill. It seemed that many members of the congregation saw Joseph's predicament as proof of what he had been all along. They now felt that he had been given a position he didn't deserve because of his grandfather, and now everybody would have to pay for it with a time-consuming search for a new associate pastor. It was only because he had no real direction in his life that Joseph had decided to enter the clergy in the first place. While he showed only minimal interest in working for the church, his relationship with Allen Shaw, Sr. had gotten him into a respectable position.

Deeply hurt by the questioning of his moral fiber, Joseph began to slowly withdraw from church involvement. Many friends urged him not to allow doubters to affect his dedication to De Angeles Memorial. Mr. Shaw begged his grandson not to be frivolous with his spiritual devotion, to continue his dedication to the church, and to possibly inquire about other positions on the faculty; but the burden became heavier with each contentious glare, and aside from that Joseph still hadn't worked up the nerve to speak with Pastor Wendell after his emotional outburst at the pastor's home. Joseph was back in that unforgiving wilderness that he had wandered in once before, hounded by guilt, unable to decide his own feelings. But this time he was not alone. He was now leading a young boy deeper and deeper into that barren place, and he would allow none of the outstretched arms of loved ones to dare try and rescue them.

Alfonzo felt more at home with Jasmine and her family than with Joseph. Every chance the youngster got he made a play to spend the night with his aunt and her two sons. Thankfully, Jasmine and her husband were more gracious than Joseph could ever have asked them to be, and they extended an open invitation to the young man.

One particular evening, when Joseph had come to pick up his son from Jasmine's home, he decided to ask a favor from his older sister. "Sis, you know I appreciate all that you and Mark have been doing for Alfonzo. He really enjoys being over here."

"You know it's not a problem. He's our family now. We enjoy having him over, and I know the boys like having him here. Can't you hear them up there?"

They hear the boys laughing and playing upstairs. Then Joseph continued. "Well, I wanted to ask you about something else. Do you think it would be okay if Alfonzo stayed here with you guys for a while, a few months or something? I mean, I know you would have to discuss it with Mark before you could tell me for sure. I just wanted you to think about it."

"Well, what's up, Joseph? Are you having some money problems or anything?"

"No, nothing like that. Everything is cool. I just need to get some things straightened out, you know."

"No I don't know. What's up? Talk to me."

"I just can't talk to the boy! It's like we're giving each other the silent treatment and we aren't even mad at each other."

"And you think having him stay over here is going to help you guys get along better?"

"I don't know, maybe? H certainly doesn't have any problem talking to you guys. I'm obviously doing something wrong."

"Joseph, you are not doing something wrong. The boy hasn't even known you for two weeks yet. What were you expecting? You guys were gonna roast marshmallows together and have campfires all night. He misses his mom. Just give him some time."

"So is that a no to him staying here?"

"Joseph, I am willing to help you. Me and Mark are willing to help you in any way we can, but sending him to stay here wouldn't be helping, it would be making things worse."

"Worse for who? Things can't get any worse for me! I already lost my position! People are talking crazy about me all over town! How is this gonna get worse?"

Jasmine wasn't accustomed to her younger brother raising his voice to her, but she didn't back down. She could feel her father's stern will taking hold of her. She was determined not to allow Joseph to slip back into the pit of despair where he had resided once before.

"So it's just about you now, is that it? Who cares about what this child might be going through! Who cares what happens to him?"

"It's me and him and his mother! About this whole situation! Why is this happening to me? I was doing fine! I was doing what I was supposed to be doing! Now everything is messed up! I can't do this!"

"Well, you had better learn to do it! And leaving him here with us ain't gonna help you learn. This is OJT, little brother, on the job training!"

Joseph decided he didn't want to hear another word. He grabbed his son's coat and turned toward the stairs to call the boy so they can leave. He quickly realized the boy had been sitting on the stairs watching and listening. He suddenly changed his tone.

"Alfonzo, come and get your coat so we can go."

Alfonzo turned and ran back up the stairs, clearly upset.

The ride home was quiet. Joseph attempted to rationalize the statements Alfonzo had overheard, but the boy remained silent.

Eventually, the tension that had resulted from the argument at Jasmine's home died down, but it was still quite apparent to both father and his son that it was not actually going away. It stayed ever present, like a dense fog throughout the house. Sometimes for a brief instant the fog would rise slightly, but then it would simply find the ceiling and soon enough return and assume its original position. It wasn't until Alfonzo's first day of school that the thick mist let loose with the rain and thunderstorms that both father and son knew it was capable of.

Kennedy Junior High School was a large, intimidating fortress of red brick. The only way on or off the campus was up the huge flight of steps and through the front entrance. The rest of the school was completely enclosed in eight-foot-high fencing. Joseph had already been to the school the day before to speak with his son's would-be instructor, and to fill out all the necessary paperwork. As the car pulled up near the front of the school, numerous children raced up, down, and around in a rush to no place in particular. They could be seen huddled in their small groups, some trying their best to be noticed, others trying equally hard not to be seen.

Joseph could feel the full measure of his son's nervousness as they both sat quietly for a moment, watching intently. He started to re-evaluate his plan not to put Alfonzo in the same school his nephews were currently attending. He would have to use Jasmine's address, which wasn't a problem, but the school was so far away. Joseph was sure he would have to depend on Jasmine and Mark's assistance to get Alfonzo back and forth to school, and after the disagreement between them it was not something he was willing to ask.

He sincerely wished that he could join Alfonzo and spend at least the first hour or two with him in class, but he knew the twelve-year-old was likely to object. Nevertheless, Dad was willing to take his shot. "You know, I can come in with you if you like and, you know, walk you to class and talk to your teacher and stuff."

Alfonzo quickly rebutted, "Uh-uh, I can go myself. This ain't no big deal. Shoot, my school back home was bigger than this one. And it had more people too." But Joseph could see the uneasiness on his son's face, clear as the sky. As Alfonzo eased out of the vehicle he glanced from one end of the school to the other, then from the top to the bottom. Joseph watched as the boy slowly climbed the steps with his backpack in hand, trying hard to portray an attitude that commanded respect.

Joseph had been home for over an hour. He had been working with his cousin Darren selling real estate. It was selling real estate that had gotten him by during the years he attended seminary. Although his faith had been shaken down to the core, he knew he had to be thankful to have a lucrative position he could quickly return to when necessary. As he sat on the couch, anxiously waiting Alfonzo's return, he flipped the television channels from one program to another, not really paying attention. Alfonzo was not all too eager to start school. Joseph had given all the advice he could conjure up, but this single listener comprised a more difficult audience than any Joseph had seen on numerous Sunday mornings.

Suddenly, he heard the front door opening, and he hoped any second to hear words of delight, or at least indifference from the new student. Instead, Alfonzo returned home with no conversation to volunteer. Instead, he made the ever-popular beeline toward his bedroom that parents of adolescents have become all too familiar with. It was clear to Joseph that the first day hadn't been extremely kind to the child. As he started to instinctively follow his son toward the bedroom, Joseph stopped and began to wonder exactly what he could say that would be most comforting. Then he felt creeping into his mind an array of things that could have gone wrong for the boy: "Could it be girls? What if he had gotten in a fight and got beaten up? What if he beat someone else up?" Suddenly he could feel all sorts of terrible thoughts overcoming him; he felt helpless. He continued to rack his brain for more answers to the even more numerous problems that could be lying in wait. Then, like a knife slicing through the center of his brain, it suddenly hit him. "I don't have the answers to all this stuff! I don't know what I'm gonna do." He turned 180 degrees and resumed his seat on the couch. With his chin resting firmly in his hand, he stared into an abysmal reality that he had not known before. Joseph found himself considering all the youthful experiences he himself had known (or thought he had known) as a boy, that nobody understood. He recalled the sit-down discussions with his father, and the type of impact, if any, they had had on an indifferent child bent on doing nothing but what tickled his fancy on any given day. It struck him that the helplessness that was now overcoming *him* was likely to have been the same helplessness that bedded down with his father on many nights, and with millions of parents around the world, for that matter. *How could this be?* he wondered. *My thirty-one years on this planet, and this is truly the first time I have considered what it must have been like to be my father. What it is like to try to impart the best of yourself to another human life.*

It seemed like only moments later when Joseph realized he had been on the couch for over an hour, pondering parenthood. Alfonzo jarred his awareness when he quietly walked through to the kitchen for an afternoon snack. Joseph strolled over, while thinking to himself, *I guess it's now or never*, and in so doing took another step toward that volatile place where parents lay their body and soul.

"So I guess it was a rough first day, huh?"

Alfonzo spoke up with his dilemma quicker than expected. This alone caused Joseph to begin to wonder if he had perhaps allowed his thoughts to wander much farther than necessary.

"Man, everybody was talking about the way I talk. They was sayin' I sound like I'm from the hillbillies and stuff!"

"Aw, man, you can't let that kind of stuff get to you. They just never heard people talk from down South. Kids are always quick to jump on somebody's case when they're different in some kind of way."

"Well, I'll tell you what! If somebody calls me hillbilly tomorrow, I'm gonna punch 'em in the face! I don't care if I get in trouble or not!"

Even though Alfonzo was still clearly upset, Joseph was somewhat relieved when he found out what the dilemma actually was. Compared to the tragic disasters that had arisen in his mind a few short moments ago, the problem of an unattractive accent seemed to be small potatoes. As he spoke, he maintained a light, pleasant tone, in an attempt to play down the severity of the situation. "Look Al, all you need to do is——"

"Al? My name is Alfonzo. Nobody ever calls me Al!"

"Well, I'm sorry. I didn't think you would mind."

The boy remained silent. Joseph took a second to think. It seemed that this minor situation was not going to be as easily dealt with as he had hoped. He decided to try to lighten the conversation as best he could. "Do you know what my father's name was?"

"Let me guess—Al."

"No, it was Allen. But people called him Al all the time. He was a good man, you know. It's never a bad idea to borrow the name of a good man."

"Well, I have my own name, and I don't want to borrow nobody else's, even if he is a good man!"

"Fine, then have it your way, no more 'Al.' But I'll tell you what. I don't want to find out you've been fighting at school over some name-calling stuff. There are only a few things in this world worth a man physically fighting somebody over, and being called a hillbilly ain't one of them!"

The discussion didn't quite go the way Joseph had envisioned. When he reluctantly phoned his sister for one of her many pieces of advice, she assured him that issues such as these are usually capable of working themselves out. And as usual, she was correct. In the coming days Joseph heard less and less about being called a hillbilly, and more and more about the various friends Alfonzo had made. Soon enough, the phone began to ring, and the cracking voices of pubescent boys crowded the phone line nightly. The kid most often ringing the phone at the Shaw residence was Shannon Marshall. Shannon had an abrupt way about him that caused Joseph to wonder if this young man was the type of company he wished for his young son. It wasn't until Shannon's first visit to the house that Joseph was assured that he wasn't.

Shannon was a sly, relaxed type of person, more relaxed in the presence of adults than most kids can ever manage to be. In his trademark green baseball cap, and worn-out, heavily-oversized jeans, Shannon was all too comfortable relaxing on his friend's living room couch with a large glass of juice he had retrieved himself. What was even more questionable was the absence of any adult supervision of the boy. Shannon rode his bicycle whenever he came over for a visit. He called at hours that Joseph felt were much too late for children of their ages, and so he promptly put a stop to it. It appeared that Shannon had free rein to roam the neighborhood as he wished. While he remained somewhat skeptical of the boy, Joseph opted not to thwart the friendship, mainly because Shannon was the first person Alfonzo had seemed to bond with since his mother's departure. It was made clear, though, that because of these reservations, any time the boys spent together would be at the Shaw home under supervision.

On one particular night, Joseph heard sounds from Alfonzo's room. The boy had gotten accustomed to spending a lot of time on the phone, but the time was long past the curfew that had been set for phone use. Joseph lay in bed for a few moments, debating the best way to approach the situation. When he finally decided he needed to take a firm approach to make certain that Alfonzo was aware that the rules were not to be ignored, he climbed out of bed and headed to the youngster's bedroom. As he approached the room, he began to realize that the sounds he was hearing were not words, but groans. Through the slightly open door, he watched as Alfonzo sat up in his bed clutching his pillow and sobbing quietly. The child's eyes were solid red as he swayed back and forth in a continuous motion.

The forty-five seconds that Joseph stood there barefoot in the hallway peering through a sliver of space may as well have been an hour. As he stood, watching in silence, the cold draft that constantly filled the area from the bathroom door past the two front bedrooms all the way to the kitchen, had no effect on him. He was enthralled in the moment. His heart went out to Alfonzo. The desperate grasp for an absent mother was something Joseph knew first hand. Not only was Alfonzo missing his mom, but he had also been removed from his grandmother who actually raised him. They had made attempts to locate the boy's grandmother in Texas, but to no avail. Joseph thought about his own nights spent in anguish in that very same room. He considered for the first time how many times his dad must have heard his crying as well, and felt the same feelings of frustration that Joseph was now feeling. He wanted so badly to come to Alfonzo's aid, but he knew that words of comfort for such a situation have not yet been created. He knew that he was helpless.

Chapter 15

When human beings become frightened or angry, they stop thinking with the forebrain. They start thinking with the midbrain which is a very primitive part of the brain. You can't rationalize with a person when he's frightened. Anybody who's ever tried to do it understands that.
    Lt. Col. Dave Grossman

She had only been back at work for two days now and already Sharonda was fed up with putting dresses back on the racks and folding V-neck shirts and turtle-neck sweaters. She couldn't stop herself from constantly checking her watch, and it seemed that time had slowed to a crawl. It had been about twenty or twenty-five minutes since her supervisor Sharon had walked by, pretending to be on her way to take care of some pressing business, but actually checking to see what various employees were up to. For that reason she knew that Sharon was due to stroll by again any minute.

Sharonda was happily surprised when her friend April made an impromptu appearance at the department store.

"Hey, girl, why you ain't called me since you got back in town? Did you track down your old college boy flame?"

"Hey, what's up, April? Yeah, I saw him. I'm not even trying to discuss him though."

April jokingly rolled her eyes at Sharonda. "Okay then, keep your little secrets then. You always were all tight lipped when it came to him anyway. You still could have called me when you got back."

"My bad girl. I ain't been doing shit since I've got back but sleeping and coming here for the last two days. What you been up to?"

"I ain't been up to nearly as much as I'm about to be. My Aunt Cheryl just sent me a plane ticket to L.A. She wants me to come out there to visit."

"You going to L.A? Damn! I wish she'd sent you two tickets. I sure wouldn't mind going out to California and not having to drive this time. I don't know how I made it back!"

"Why don't you come with me? All you need to do is pay for a ticket. We're gonna stay at my aunt's house, so you won't have to pay for no hotel and probably not any food either."

Sharonda ceased pretending to fold clothes and turned her full attention to April as she responded. "Are you serious?"

"Yes, I'm serious!"

"Ooh, you know, that would be nice! I've never been to L.A. I don't know though. You know my mom is still in the hospital. I think I might need to be here in case anything happens. I haven't even been by to see her since I got back."

"Come on, Sharonda! I don't leave for almost two weeks. That's more than enough time for you to visit with your mother and get your ticket. You know, you could use a little time away anyways. We'll stay out there for a couple weeks and you'll be ready for whatever after that."

"You know, you're right. I can't let my girl go out to L.A. by herself. Call me up tonight and let me know what flight you're on so I can book a ticket. We're about to be up and out into the sunshine you know!"

Just then Sharonda caught sight of Sharon walking by. She grabbed a shirt and pretended to be looking for the proper place for the garment. April recognized the game and pretended to be shopping. Sharon glanced at Sharonda, then looked April up and down closely before moving on. When she was finally out of sight, Sharonda continued, "I can't stand her! I might not even tell this stupid job that I'm leaving. I might just disappear and find another job when I get back. If I tell them I need a couple weeks, I know they're gonna start trippin'. I'm tired of them anyways!"

"You do what you gotta do."

"I know that's right. I think I'm gonna go by the hospital tonight to see my mom. Why don't you come with me? She would probably like to see your crazy butt if she's awake."

"Aw, you know I would, but I'm supposed to be spending the night with Andre. You know, he's all trippin' cause I'm going away for a couple weeks. Every five minutes he's like (in a mocking deep voice), Why you gotta go to L.A. though? Don't be out there talking to no dudes!"

The two laughed at April's imitation, before she continued on. "Tell your mom I said hi though. I hope she gets better."

"Thanks. I'll tell her."

"So I'll call you tonight and give you my flight number. We're about to go and turn Cali out, girl!"

The ladies shared a hug before April started to walk off. After taking a few steps, she turned back to mention a final point to her friend. "You know, you got to let a sister know if you really decide to let this job go. I might need to come and pick up some outfits on your discount so I can set it off on the West Coast. Payday is just around the corner."

Sharonda giggled and waved to April. "You're right. If I leave, where am I gonna buy *my* clothes? Maybe I'd better stay a little longer."

After the departure of her friend, Sharonda began to daydream about going to Los Angeles, but the dreams didn't last long. Soon, her thoughts drifted to her mother and the hospital. She had been putting off a visit to the hospital in every way possible, making one excuse after another why each night was a bad night. She hadn't been able to reach her dad, and now she knew she would have to go alone.

On the drive over she picked up a magazine, some chips, and a soda. Last time she was at the hospital she got nervous and couldn't figure out what to do with her hands. Although she was there for a mere forty-five minutes, it felt like hours. At first she hoped her mom would be awake. If they could talk a little, at least the time would go faster. But after she thought about it a little more, she figured it would be better if her mom were asleep. Mom's first words would most likely be "How is Alfonzo?" This was a question Sharonda would certainly rather not be forced to respond to at present.

As she walked down the hospital corridor, she could hear a woman moaning and complaining. "I don't need to go with you! Why are you trying to take me out of my bed? I don't need to go anywhere with you!"

South Stanton Community Hospital was not known as one of the better hospitals in Texas. It had a poor reputation, and Sharonda worried for her mom's care. The nurses often seemed lethargic and short-tempered, but Patty, a Mexican woman who was her mom's nurse, didn't fit the mold; Patty was very helpful. When Sharonda reached her mom's room, Patty was inside hard at work. When she caught sight of Sharonda, Patty greeted her warmly. Sharonda was surprised the nurse remembered her so easily.

"Hi, how you doing tonight? I see you coming to check on Momma, huh."

Sharonda just shyly responded, "Yeah."

Being an attentive nurse, Patty would have certainly noticed that Sharonda hadn't been to visit in over a week. Sharonda braced herself for the casual criticisms that she was an uncaring daughter, but the criticisms never came. Patty just kept chatting on about how well Momma had been doing in recent days.

"Momma was awake a little while ago; you just missed her. You wait here awhile. She might wake up again. I bet she be happy to see you."

Sharonda just smiled and nodded. She was thankful not to be forced to create an excuse for her absence.

Patty continued going about her routine. As Sharonda watched, she hoped the nurse wouldn't finish. Then she would be left alone with just her mom. Last time she tried talking to her mom as she lay unconscious. It felt weird, almost unnatural. She wasn't sure if she should try that again or not. What would she say anyways? The two hadn't talked very much prior to the stroke. Why should things change now that she lay in a hospital bed?

But just then Sharonda's fear was realized. The nurse was finishing up and was heading out the door. Patty had been a nurse for a long time, and could tell that Sharonda was having trouble with the situation. Before leaving she gave some suggestions to the hesitant visitor.

"Ven aqui, here, you sit down right here and talk to Momma."

Patty placed a chair right next to the bed.

"We mommas like to hear from our daughters. You tell her all about you day today or another day."

Sharonda could do nothing but smile and say okay. As she sat in the chair, she saw her mom a lot closer than she had before. The last time she visited she sat across the room and only came close to say hi and bye. Now, sitting next to the bed, she looked closely at her mother. She looked older, much older. Her hair was graying and her skin wasn't as smooth as it had been in the recent past. Sharonda felt the fear for her mom that she didn't feel during the last visit. Her mom was getting older, and things would have to change, whether June Atkins would ever leave South Stanton Hospital or not. For the first time in a long time, Sharonda considered the fact that she and her mom really had no other family. June had been an only child, and so had Sharonda. They never had much of a relationship with her father's side of the family, and her maternal grandparents were dead. If her mom died, Sharonda would be alone. She had to say something, but what?

"Mom, Mom it's me, Sharonda."

Sharonda mustered up the courage to gingerly reach her hand over and stroke the hair from her mom's face. Once she was able to feel the gray strands sliding through her fingers, she felt the need to continue the motion.

"Mom, I just wanted to see how you've been doing."

She paused, looking around the room, as if the next words to say were placed somewhere on the walls.

"You know, your nurse Patty seems really nice. She reminds me of that lady that used to work at that liquor store down the street from our first house, remember? She used to always be talking to me and I didn't even know what she was saying. I wonder if she's still at that store. April came by my job today. I hadn't seen her in a while. She's still crazy. She wanted to come by, but she had to do something with her stupid boyfriend. I think Jahlan might come by when she gets back from wherever she went. Last time I talked to her she asked about you. You know, she thinks you're her second mother."

Sharonda took a sip of Pepsi and thought about whether or not she should say what was next on her mind.

"Mom, I tried to call Daddy. He didn't answer, but I left a message for him. I don't know if he's gonna call back or not. He has some dumb old '70s song on his answering machine. He's still stuck in the '70s. Somebody needs to tell him we're in the new millennium now. I told him what hospital you're in. If he comes by, I hope I'm not here."

Sharonda thought hard, trying to imagine what her mom might say in response to some of the comments being made. She knew her mom was also a fan of '70s music. She also knew her mom would be concerned about the well-being of her daughter and grandson above all else.

"Mom, I'm doing all right, so you don't have to worry about me or Alfonzo. We're both fine. He does miss you, though. We both know that boy ain't no good without his Granny."

After another long pause, Sharonda said what had been rolling around in her head for years: "Mom we love you. You know Alfonzo loves you, and I love you too. You gotta get out of this place. When you do, I'll be right there. I'm sorry I'm always complaining about stuff. I just wish you would let me make my own mistakes sometimes. You always want to save me from everything. I don't want to be saved. I just want to go and try things sometimes. But I thank you for caring. We both know Daddy don't."

Sharonda stared at her mom's face. She appeared to be resting peacefully. Lying flat on her back, with her mouth slightly open and an I V running into her arm, she still looked more peaceful than on a normal day in the life of June Atkins. Sharonda sat back in her chair and pulled out her magazine. She read a little, and looked through the pictures while nibbling on her snacks. Two hours later she kissed her mom goodbye and walked out.

As Sharonda walked down the hall she heard her name called.

"Ms. Atkins. Hi how are you? I'm Dr. Taylor. I was hoping I could speak to you about your mom."

Sharonda didn't really want to speak to him. Something about him made her nervous. She wondered how he knew who she was. Maybe the overzealous nurse filled him in? She responded to his question in a tone that would hopefully make her appear to be in a hurry.

"Um, sure." Looking at her watch.

Even though he may have gotten her message the doctor was not about to let her out of the conversation.

"We can walk as we talk if you like."

The two headed down the hall toward the elevators as he continued.

"I haven't had the opportunity to speak with you since your mom was admitted."

Sharonda began hoping that the conversation was not leading toward finances. She had no idea what her mom's financial status was, and she had no way of paying for medical bills herself. She quickened her pace and made no eye contact with Dr. Taylor as he continued speaking.

"I just want to make certain you are aware of the seriousness of your mom's condition."

Sharonda stopped.

"Seriousness? How serious is it?"

"I'm afraid it's very serious. We have done just about all we can for your mom. At this point we are pretty much just trying to keep her comfortable."

The ease with which he made the statement made Sharonda feel that maybe she had misunderstood him.

"Comfortable for what? You don't mean so she can die!"

"I mean there isn't much else we can do for her. I'm sorry"

Sharonda stood silent for a few seconds. She wasn't sure what to say or do. As she stood there she realized that she actually had already felt in her heart what the doctor was telling her. Now she could no longer ignore the dire circumstances. She could no longer pretend that things were not as they were. She then asked the obvious question.

"How long do you think she has?"

"I really can't say, maybe a few days, maybe a few months? It's really out of our control at this point."

Sharonda looked away then stepped onto the elevator. Dr. Taylor attempted to continue the conversation.

"Ms. Atkins there are still a few details that we need to discuss. I need to know what you would like us to do in certain situations."

Sharonda simply pressed the button and allowed the elevator doors to close. She started to cry but the elevator quickly stopped for others to get in. She couldn't bare to let strangers see her cry. She fought back the tears all the way to the parking lot.

Sharonda made two more visits to her mom the following week. Aside from her daughter, the only other people to visit June Atkins were a couple of friends and associates from the church she attended. They made a number of infrequent visits when they would sit and either talk or read to her.

On the 12th day after making plans with April, Sharonda packed her bags and headed for the airport. As she waited at the designated terminal to board her flight Sharonda sat beside a young white lady. The lady was on her cell phone and Sharonda couldn't help overhearing the conversation.

"I'll be back in a couple of weeks. I'll take a lot of pictures for you. Yes mom I will call you as soon as I get there. I know you'll be up because you're always up at midnight. I love you too. Goodbye."

The young lady's patience was clearly wearing thin, but Sharonda couldn't help thinking about her own mom. She couldn't help but compare the impatience she had always shown to her. Sharonda watched a little girl walking through the airport, hand in hand with her mother, joy and appreciation bubbling forth in every stride the child took. Sharonda looked at the plane ticket in her hand. She thought about her mom lying probably alone in a hospital bed only a few miles away. She thought about the words of Dr. Taylor and the uncertainty of her mom's days. She felt an impulse to leave the airport, to get in her car and go to her mother's bedside. She stood up and as if on cue Sharonda heard the voice of the ticket agent over the loud speaker,

"We are now boarding for flight #721 to Los Angeles."

April trotted up to Sharonda's side refreshed from the restroom. April assumed her friend had stood up to board the plane. She grabbed Sharonda's hand.

"Let's go girl! It's about time they started boarding. Don't forget you promised I would get the window seat."

Sharonda handed her ticket to the agent and didn't look back.

Chapter 16

There was no need to explain what Hell was: I had already done "time" there. For these few hours had been enough to show me that everywhere was Hell where Christ was not.
Paul Claudel

As the Shaw house was quiet on a particular Friday evening, Alfonzo was surprised to hear the sound of continuous rapping on his bedroom window. As he gazed through half-startled and half-sleepy eyes, he realized that it was his buddy Shannon trying to get his attention. Joseph looked at the alarm clock, which read 11:50, and he looked back at the window in total amazement. His friend motioned for him to get up and come to him, but it took the sleepy boy a couple more seconds to become fully aware. Shannon suggested to Alfonzo that the two of them take a Friday night out and head down to the arcade only a few miles away. Alfonzo was clearly hesitant. He knew his father had bunked down on the couch for the night watching his favorite movie of all time, *Stormy Weather*. It was likely, but not certain, that Joseph would sleep there for the night. But it was also quite possible that Dad might wake up and decide to retire to his own bedroom, and on the way he would be sure to check in on his young son.

Shannon did all he could to convince his friend that Friday night at the arcade was just what he needed to boost his reputation at school.

"All of the in-kids from school are always at the arcade on Friday night. We'll only stay for about an hour at the most, and then we'll come on home. I don't want you to get caught, but I'm telling you: If all the kids from school see you at the arcade on a Friday night, you're in like Flynn. Nobody's gonna be calling you hillbilly no more."

The decision was all but made. But still, Alfonzo felt it necessary to take just one quick glance into the living room to see how comfortable old Dad appeared to be bunked down on that couch. As he peered through a partially open door, he could see Joseph all bundled up. There was a cup of once-steaming hot tea, now turned lukewarm, sitting directly in front of him, and although his much-adored Lena Horne was sensuously serenading him, he answered her with grating snores. Alfonzo joined his friend, convinced that if Lena was unable to stimulate Dad's awareness, then the concerns of a midnight arising were unfounded. Alfonzo quickly got dressed, and the two sped off, joyously sharing a ride on Shannon's bike, both in mounting anticipation of the exciting time to come at the legendary downtown arcade.

As the boys rode, it became more and more apparent to Alfonzo that they were no longer in the cozy town of De Angeles. They had entered Sacramento sometime ago, and were now nearing downtown. He saw increasing numbers of people strolling about the streets, and numerous lights brightening up the storefronts. He knew their destination couldn't be much farther away. They passed a number of places that he had remembered seeing out the window of the car as he rode about town running errands with his dad. There was the bowling alley, and the mall. There was the movie theater that he still couldn't believe had twenty-five movie screens inside of it. There was certainly no downtown like this back home.

As they turned onto the final street, Alfonzo was amazed at the monstrous sign lit up in what had to be fifty different colors: "8th Street Arcade." He was giddy.

The tiny voice in his head, accusing him of blatant deceitfulness, was giving way to a myriad of other thoughts. Soon, what had once been the agonizing chore of going to school, would become an utter joy, as his newfound schoolyard reputation was to be catapulted directly into the Kennedy Junior High Hall of Fame. While the squeaky bicycle pulled Alfonzo closer and closer toward his presumed destiny, he began surveying the area for various schoolmates who had already made a name for themselves among the student body. What he noticed was not what he had envisioned. Among the lively mass of people crowded around conversing outside of the establishment, not only were those key BMOCs—the Big Men on Campus—not to be found, but Alfonzo didn't recognize anybody. There wasn't one person from Kennedy to be found anywhere. While obviously disappointed, Alfonzo wasn't quite ready to relinquish all the majestic myths he had conjured up only moments before. He assured himself that all of the people Shannon had mentioned must already be inside. After all, it was past midnight already. Even better, this was just about the perfect time for a fashionably late entry. All of the nerds will have had to leave a long time ago. Showing up in the early morning hours had to be worth a few cool points.

But as the two confidently stepped into what was supposed to be pay dirt, Alfonzo quickly realized that his fantasies of grandeur would likely remain fantasies. What he expected to be a bustling place of people talking, laughing, and playing, was nothing more than a quaint group of strangers who appeared to have nothing better to do on a Friday night. Shannon, for some reason, didn't appear all too bothered by the lack of familiar faces that greeted them. He quickly scoped out his favorite game, and ushered his buddy over to watch as he displayed his virtuosity. As he stood idly by watching the game, Alfonzo could hear the voice returning which had pestered him for most of the bicycle ride. He began to wonder about the possibilities of being caught in such an outright act of disobedience. He had never really done anything to warrant a serious punishment from his new father. In the unfortunate possibility that Lena happened to revive her audience, just what type of punishment could be waiting back at home? Fear began to simmer. Alfonzo snapped at his friend,

"Man, is this it? There ain't nobody here but old people and hippies! I can't believe we came down here for this!"

Without lifting his eyes from the video game screen, Shannon casually responded,

"I know man, I don't know what happened. There's usually a lot of people from school here."

After twenty minutes of watching Shannon shoot down oncoming ships, Alfonzo finally gave way to his fears, which were now bubbling over inside. "Man, there ain't nobody coming here from school! I got to go home before my dad wakes up! Shannon assured his friend that as soon as his last two quarters were gone he would be ready to go. Alfonzo waited impatiently. As he watched the game, he began to silently root for the oncoming alien ships to make short work of his buddy. As Alfonzo again surveyed his surroundings, it became apparent to him that the two of them were clearly the youngest patrons there. The fear of what awaited him at home was gradually being joined by the fear of being so far away from home in such a questionable place. There were people smoking marijuana in the corner. In another corner, there were a guy and a girl kissing much more passionately than seemed appropriate. With each passing second it became more and more apparent to him that he had indeed made a bad decision to ever leave his warm bed.

At last the aliens had won, and at least this portion of the nightmare appeared to be drawing to a close. The youngsters made their way to the exit with an impatient Alfonzo leading the way. As they stepped into the night air, Alfonzo was taken aback.

"Where did you leave your bike?"

Shannon replied, equally troubled,

"I left it right here, didn't I?"

The boys looked around every possible place they could think of, but to no avail. The bike was gone.

Suddenly the fear was no longer bubbling over, but exploding forth. Alfonzo began to shout,

"I can't believe this! What happened to the bike? What are we gonna do?" He made a vague attempt at disguising his tears, but they were coming at too strong a force to be hidden. Shannon by now was also in an obvious state of peaked emotions. He shouted various obscenities and glared up and down the street, in a hopeless attempt to catch sight of the perpetrator. A number of older youths chuckled to themselves and others, as they watched the two frenzied boys.

As Alfonzo and Shannon worried and talked, it soon became plain that each of them had very different concerns. Shannon was angry about the loss of his most valued property, while Alfonzo, on the other hand, was almost exclusively worried about how to get home, and what might very well be waiting for him when he got there. Each of them berated the other for not acknowledging the most serious problem, then they stopped speaking to each other altogether. It was only after nearly ten minutes had passed that the two hard-luck travelers realized that they had a good distance to walk ahead of them, and that it would be a shorter walk if they did it together. As they started off, Alfonzo told himself that he would not cry again until he was safely in his bed and out of the sight of his traveling companion.

The time was now past 1:30 in the morning. As they walked, Alfonzo noticed many things he hadn't noticed on the ride in. There were many bars up and down the streets, some of them with the doors wide open so you could see right inside as plain as day as you went by. Also, there were plenty of adults walking about. He found it strange that none of them seemed to pay any attention to two twelve-year-old boys walking around downtown at this late hour. Even the women that walked past acted as though the two boys were invisible. At one point they saw a police car driving down the street directly in their path. Okay, now they were both sure that they were about to take a ride in the black and white vehicle, like it or not. But the car just cruised on by without so much as a glance from the officers inside. Neither of them knew what to make of it. They both just kept their heads down and continued on in the direction of their homes.

When they heard a car pull up close behind them playing loud music, the two boys purposely made an attempt not to look up, but to keep walking. It wasn't until they heard a deep voice call Shannon by name that they looked behind them to see just who was trying to get their attention. Shannon looked relieved when he saw the shiny green car nearly on the curb.

"Aw, man, it's Bobby!"

"Bobby? Who's Bobby?"

"That's my sister's friend Bobby! He's cool." Shannon eagerly trotted over to the car to speak with the older Bobby. Alfonzo still held back.

Bobby was a twenty-six-year-old ex-boyfriend of Shannon's now eighteen-year-old sister. Although the two were only together for a few short months, Shannon had always had a fascination for the flashy cars and clothes Bobby was accustomed to owning. Bobby and another male passenger chit-chatted with Shannon for a few moments while Alfonzo remained out of earshot. Then Shannon turned to his friend, and motioned for him to come to the car.

"They're gonna give us a ride home, man, come on!" Alfonzo remained reluctant. He continued to examine the car and the riders in the car as he inched forward.

"Are you sure? They don't know where I live." Shannon quickly shot down Alfonzo's excuses and insisted that they would be fools to pass up the opportunity with such a long way to go. Finally Alfonzo agreed, after considering his friend's point.

Inside the car he could barely hear Shannon talking to him, the music was up so loud. All he could hear from the front seat was a few jumbled words and some occasional laughter. Bobby then turned down the stereo and addressed the boys.

"What you two shorties doing out here in the middle of the night, anyway? Shannon, I know you're going to get an ass whooping if your mother catches you out here! Y'all lucky me and Jay had a run to make, or your little scary asses would've been hoofing it all the way home." When Shannon explained to the two men that his bicycle had been stolen, they both burst out in laughter. They agreed that it was a lesson that the boys should stay home during the late night hours. Bobby then informed the two youngsters that he and his friend had a quick stop to make. It would only take a few moments, and then they would take them on to their respective homes.

As the dark green Nova rumbled down one dimly-lit back road after another through the most hidden parts of the capital city, Alfonzo sat engulfed in a prolonged state of uneasiness. This night, which had begun with the highest expectations, had now become one in which to be able to climb into bed and forget it ever happened would be the best possible outcome. At every turn, the circumstances appeared to be taking a tumble, further and further downhill. He only hoped that this impromptu cruise through some of the dingier parts of the city wouldn't continue the downward spiral.

When the car finally slowed to a stop in front of some brick-looking apartment houses, the boys figured they were one step nearer to the end of this tumultuous night. Shannon had gradually changed his attitude from excitement to concern. His voice showed his worry over whether they had made the best decision in accepting the ride, but he clearly wasn't ready to express his doubts. He still tried to assure Alfonzo that everything was going to be fine.

"Man, I can't wait to get home. This is whack, I better not never find out who took my bike or it's gonna be on!" But Alfonzo was hardly listening. He was far too concerned about his own fate, which he somehow sensed was growing dimmer by the second.

Bobby and his friend exited the car and told the boys to sit tight; they would be right back. As the boys sat quietly in the back seat of the car, they were both confronted by the sudden, extreme silence that replaced the high-powered stereo system that had blared at them on the drive over. There was now only one poorly lit streetlight nearby, and no pedestrians crowding the sidewalks. Now there were only the sounds of this darkest of nights—the sounds of crickets chirping, and an occasional car motoring by far off in the distance. With the windows down, they could feel the cool night air. It seemed to have a bit more chill than it had earlier in the evening while they were walking, perhaps because they had managed to work up a little sweat as they marched.

Neither of the boys talked much as they sat and waited. One would intermittently ask some vague question or make some casual conversation, if only to briefly break the silence, but for the most part it was the silence itself that spoke the loudest. It was the type of silence that arises inside dire circumstances.

After nearly twenty minutes of sitting quietly, the boys were growing impatient. Shannon was beginning to complain, and Alfonzo had to go to the bathroom. When Shannon suggested his pal make use of the bushes across the street, Alfonzo admitted that he would appreciate his friend's company, since the bushes in question were so far off. Shannon agreed, and the two boys eased out of the vehicle and gingerly ambled across the street to the dense brown bushes.

As Alfonzo relieved himself, he heard Shannon whisper that he believed he saw Bobby and his friend finally returning. Alfonzo whispered back to Shannon, "Wait for me, man, don't just leave me over here in these bushes by myself!"

"What's wrong? You scared the boogie man gonna show up and grab you by your ding-a-ling?" While laughing to himself, Shannon realized that he didn't see *two* people coming toward the car, he saw three. As he quietly relayed the information to his buddy, who was just about finishing up, the two wondered why there would be three individuals. Alfonzo finally zipped up his jeans, and turned to witness for himself what appeared to be three dark forms approaching the car across the street. Before he could say a word, he saw the individual walking farthest behind draw a handgun from his pants and fire two bullets at point-blank range directly into the man in front of him. The two boys, now gripped with fear, had surprisingly similar reactions. Nearly frozen, they both slowly backed into the bushes, although they each desperately wanted to run. Breathing deeply and quickly, Shannon clutched Alfonzo's arm. Alfonzo opened his mouth and heard himself making faint moans. He tried to speak, but only the moans came out. Instinct told them it was likely that the gunman would hear them fleeing, and possibly turn his attention to them. So they remained there, frozen.

As the individual who had been walking farthest in front turned and saw the gun pointed directly toward him, he began desperately pleading for his life. Just witnessing such frantic shouts of hopelessness from a grown man enveloped the boys even more deeply in fear. It was apparent, even in the shrieks of the surreal milliseconds, that the voice was familiar. It was Bobby, pleading for his life in some blurry, barely discernible rhetoric.

"Look, D, c'mon, man! You know I wouldn't do you and Damian like that. You can't do this, man."

The gunman slowly walked toward his prey, and as he became more illuminated by the streetlight hanging overhead they could see his blue jeans and shiny black leather vest. His hair was in long braids and his jewelry glistened in the moonlight. His voice was full of rage as he just kept repeating his empty question, "Now what, now what you got to say, huh, now what?" The man's heavily tattooed arm was outstretched and now was only a few feet away from the forehead of Bobby Humphreys. Bobby shook his head continually and finally lowered his now-soaked tightly squeezed eyes toward the ground. Whether his next words were going to be an altered plea for *this* life, or a surrendering prayer for the next, will never be known. Mr. Humphreys was pushed down and onto his side by a violent flurry of bullets that became academic after the first two had been discharged.

It was out of a mountain of sheer luck that the offender backed away as he fired, and in the blink of an eye he had dashed off into the darkness. The cold silence that had engulfed the young boys quickly turned into wails of panic. Surely the gunman would have been made aware of his unwanted company had he stuck around any longer. The boys' hands remained cupped over their ears in a vain attempt to drown out the deafening blasts. It was only after many seconds had passed that Shannon grabbed Alfonzo's arm and physically suggested they both vacate the premises. And vacate they did, as far and as fast as they could. As the tears streamed down their faces, neither made even the slightest attempt to wipe them away. Shannon fled at top speed, and Alfonzo, desperate not to be left behind, stayed hot on his trail. Had it not been so very late at night, some passerby would certainly have discerned an emergency and come to the aid of the two.

The boys soon realized that simply running was not going to completely rectify their now horrid predicament. They had no idea how to get home, and they had less than two dollars between them. Punishment considered, they both knew a call had to be made and, frankly, Alfonzo's still-undersized fingers couldn't dial the number fast enough to suit the two youngsters.

Minutes later, Joseph Shaw found himself on an empty road. He was driving toward a specific street on the other side of town. His thoughts were far away from the maneuverings of the vehicle. They were all bound up in a tightly spun knot, clinging to a boy whom a few short months ago he hadn't even known existed. When he found the two boys standing on the curbside, slumped over as if it were painful to even stand up, he stopped the car.

Although affection had eluded their relationship for the most part, the embrace of father and son that followed was lengthy and intense for both. Joseph softly whispered to his boy,

"Thank God, thank God! I was so worried about you. I don't know what I would have done."

As he ushered them into the vehicle Joseph firmly demanded both an explanation and an exact account of what had transpired. Sirens could be heard descending on the neighborhood, and although he had a strong suspicion that the boys had some sort of tie-in with them, he chose to continue driving. When the whole terrifying story had finally been recounted, he was in awe. His emotions had run the gamut from anger, to disbelief, to utter despair.

He took Shannon home and explained what had happened to Ms. Marshall in the fewest words he could manage. Although Denise Marshall was surprised, her reaction was mild, in Joseph's opinion. Standing in the doorway in her red nightgown as he spoke, she never even bothered to put down her cigarette. After handing her wayward son a quick smack to the back of the head, and ordering him to bed, she simply thanked Joseph for returning the boy and told him goodnight. Joseph by then was emotionally drained, as was his son, and Joseph desired only to go home and deal with this night in the morning.

Chapter 17

Iron sharpeneth iron; so a man sharpeneth the countenance of his friend.
Proverbs 27:17

Morning came sooner than it was requested. Joseph found himself sitting at the kitchen table catching a glimpse of the bright sun, lower than most Saturday mornings allow. He was completely engulfed in uncertainty as he waited for Alfonzo to emerge from his room. Alfonzo had suffered enough already for his transgressions. There would be no further punishment, at least none to be inflicted by his father. But what of Bobby Humphreys and Greg May, the two men who lay dead in the street? What of their families? What of their assailant? To leave things as they were, with the possibility of justice in reach, but not pursued, would be not only wrong but evil as well. Joseph could hear his father's words as if he were at the table beside him: "Fear and indifference are two of the biggest threats to righteousness man can ever come up against. A man may as well have the devil on his team as partner with a scared Christian!" Well, both fear and indifference had found their way to the Shaw residence this morning, and they refused to go. Joseph surfed the channels on the small, thirteen-inch television set in search of local news that might shed some light on last night's incident.

At last, Alfonzo gingerly crept into the kitchen and quietly poured himself a bowl of cereal. With the television volume down to almost nothing, the room remained quiet. When he was finally convinced that he would find no local news, Joseph turned off the set and turned his attention to his son.

"I have to ask you this question, and I want you to think hard about the answer before you give it to me, okay?" After receiving the nod of approval, he continued. "How well did you see the guy who shot those two young men last night?"

After sitting in apparent meditation for a few short seconds, Alfonzo spoke up. "I saw what he was wearing, and I saw the tattoo on his arm—of a cross—I think."

"You think—did you see the cross or not?"

"I don't know."

"Was there anything else? Did you see anything else, or hear anything else?"

Alfonzo thought hard. "The guy with the gun just kept saying, 'Now what you gonna do, now what?' That guy, Bobby, was real scared. I couldn't tell most of what he was saying, but one time I heard him say, 'C'mon, D, you know I wouldn't do that to you and da man.'"

"Are you sure, 'C'mon, D, I wouldn't do that to you and da man?'"

"Yeah, but he said it kind of funny, like, 'you and da meean.'"

"'Da meean?' What are you talking about? Are you sure that's what he said?"

"I don't know. That's what it sounded like."

Joseph tried hard to hide his feelings, both from Alfonzo and from himself, but the truth was he didn't much like the answers to his questions. He left the room, and after he was out of Alfonzo's sight, began to pace as he thought. The last fleeting piece of hope that he desperately clung to was the possibility that the perpetrator had already been apprehended, or at least identified, in which case nobody from the Shaw family need get involved. Should he call somebody, or maybe just call the police department? What to do? After mulling over the question for over fifteen minutes, he turned the television set back on to find the answer to his question. Two men had indeed been killed, and there were no current suspects in the case.

Oh, God, please, no! Joseph was overcome with distress. *How can this be happening?* Now, staring him and his new addition to the Shaw lineage squarely in the heart, was the indebtedness that binds all Christians. The indebtedness that is only brought forth when following God causes one to choose the life-endangering road that could easily be avoided were it not for that promise. He went into his room and shut the door. As he sat down on the bed and clutched a pillow, he could hear the demons begin to softly reason with him. Would it really be a smart thing to put your son and yourself in that kind of situation? Nobody can bring them back now except God. If it's that important, why not let God bring them back, and leave you and yours alone. Like every other man, they reap what they sow, so they surely had it coming.

It was urgent that he talk to somebody. Joseph knew that his mind and heart were quickly withering away, leaving only bitter resentment. After dropping Alfonzo with Aunt Jasmine, he met his old friend James Quincy downtown for lunch.

It had been weeks since the two had talked. In the past, it was worthy of concern when more than a couple of days passed without at least a phone call. James was happy to be meeting with Joseph, and right away he offered to pick up the tab. The restaurant was a favorite of theirs, famous around town for the black-eyed peas and sweet potatoes, but James was mildly disappointed when his crony ordered only salad and iced tea. The conversation was dragging along much slower than was the custom for the two until James inquired about the fatherhood that had befallen his friend. Joseph somberly made it clear that it was indeed this fatherhood that had caused him to request today's lunch date. After preparing him for the gravity of the story to follow, Joseph told James of the tragic events that had occurred the previous night. James winced in despair with each detail until finally he cried out in anguish, "Oh, my God," briefly causing a scene before the other diners. James had read about the shootings in the paper and couldn't get over the shock of the news. He had assumed that Joseph must be having a difficult time, since he hadn't seen or spoken to him in such a long time, but he never would have dreamed something as major as these events would have happened.

Joseph was silent. Part of him was still in shock himself, part of him was ashamed for his son. James did the best he could as a comforter, but it was obvious that he was at a loss for words. Over and over again he reinforced how amazed he was. Then, after falling silent himself for a short but uncomfortable amount of time, he finally asked the one question that had been lingering in the back of his mind: "How well did he really see the shooter?" After a deep sigh, Joseph replied, "I think he got a pretty good look at him." They began discussing all of the pros and cons of allowing Alfonzo to speak to the police. Although they came up with a far lengthier list of the latter, their consciences still surrounded them, ravaging one excuse after the next. There duty lay, as vast as the ocean, able to submerge the soundest reasoning and leave it scattered about its floor. Their consciences were indicting. Their moral and ethical sense of dedication to truth could not be held captive.

Joseph leaned forward on his elbows and allowed his mind to go back to happier times. "You know if it would have been me that witnessed something like that my mom would have dragged me straight down to the police station to tell what I saw. She wouldn't even have hesitated."

"What would your dad have said?"

"He would have said, 'Boy you better do what your momma says!'"

"Ha! Yeah, your mom was no joke."

"She was only about five foot two, and my pops was all big and hard, but people didn't know that she was the one that ran the house."

"Oh, I believe it! Your mom was for real. Did I ever tell you what she did to me when I was thirteen?"

"No. What did she do?"

"Man, I thought I told you about that. You remember Natalie Saunders?"

"Who?"

"Natalie Saunders. She used to run with your sister Jasmine all the time. It would be her, Natalie and Ramona."

"Oh, Natalie that was always dressed to kill."

"Yeah, there you go. When I was thirteen your mom caught me and Natalie kissing in the choir room at the church.

"What! I never heard that!"

"You was just a little crumb snatcher back then. Man, let me tell you, when your mom busted us I thought I was gonna pee in my pants. All I could stand there and say was "please don't tell my mamma! Please don't tell my mamma!"

"I bet you did. Your mom would have whooped your behind and then let the pastor whoop you too."

"I know it. But your mom was cool. She just looked at me and said, 'Alright I won't tell your mom.' I thought I was in the clear, but before she walked away she said, 'But that don't mean I won't tell anybody else.'"

"What did she mean by that?"

"That's what I was wondering! I'm thinking, she ain't gonna tell the pastor on me is she? Man, I got to church the next Sunday right. I'm sitting in the back row while everybody is supposed to be praying right. All of a sudden I feel this heavy hand on my shoulder. I look up and it's Mr. Saunders, Natalie's dad looking down at me. This man leans down and whispers in my ear, 'If I ever find out you had your lips on my daughter again, it's gonna take more that prayer to keep my hands from around your neck. Do you hear me, son?' Brother I was froze!"

"My mom busted you out like that?"

"Like that! I was so scared I couldn't even answer the man. And he whispered it so smooth too. My parents were sitting right next to me and they never heard a thing. Your mom did me wrong, but she knew that was what I needed. I tell you I never looked twice at Natalie again. That's for sure."

"I've never heard that story before."

"I just assumed Jasmine told you. Yeah, your mom was good people. She's one of those people who took the high road to Heaven."

"The high road?"

"The high road, man. She's one of those people that actually tried to do what she was supposed to be doing. To put God first."

Joseph was somewhat intrigued by the terminology. He had never heard the term *high road to Heaven* before.

"I mean, it's not like she was perfect, but even when I was little I could tell that she took God seriously and tried to do the right things. My uncle used to say that people who lived like that took the high road to Heaven. He said they showed up to Heaven with a few less lumps on their noggin. Not like most of us. Even if we do make it into the gates, we take that low road. We take that road where we don't learn our lessons the first time around. We need to be taught over and over and over. We go fumbling, stumbling, and bumbling, along that narrow path trying to hold on to the controls, you know?"

"And we show up with the extra knots on our head to prove it."

"Ain't that the truth?"

Joseph's thoughts turned back to his son. Something had to be done. He knew they couldn't just walk away.

The longer they sat it became increasingly apparent that a strenuous and rocky road was just around the bend. James wanted to do more, to be of more use, but he knew the assistance he could provide was limited. After plenty of intense searching for any possible way he could be of more substantial help, James finally came up with something that could very well alleviate some of Joseph's fear. He had a friend who worked for the local police department. Michael Kelley had been a buddy to James for a number of years now, and had proven himself to be a very trusting and compassionate man. It was James' hope that maybe they could get Michael to give them some idea, off the record of course, of how the case against the offender was progressing. Maybe they could tell Michael what it was that Alfonzo saw, and he in turn could give them an idea of how important it would actually be for the boy to go on record with his information. Maybe what he saw would be of no help at all. Maybe they already knew who did it, and just weren't letting the public in on the details yet. Joseph was a little skeptical at first, but he knew his options were limited.

Before they left, Joseph gave his consent to have James set up a meeting with the police officer.

Joseph wasn't home long before he called Jasmine to find out if Alfonzo could once again stay the night. She consented, but then pressed Joseph to find out what had been bothering her younger brother. He convinced her it was nothing, that he just desperately needed an evening to himself. For the rest of the day, Joseph sat in front of the television. He flipped channels from this to that, complaining to himself that nothing was on. With so much anxious energy, he continued walking back and forth to the neighborhood store for junk food. At last, when night came, he decided to head out to Shari's for a simple dinner.

Sitting alone in the booth, Joseph ate slowly, wondering if passersby felt pity for this lonely diner. He desperately wanted dessert, but wasn't inclined to sit there alone any longer. As he waited for the waitress to wrap up his doggy bag, Joseph heard his name being called. It was Jonathan Blackwell.

"J Shaaaaaaw, what's up, man? What you doin' up in here all by yourself looking all lonely and shit?"

"Jonathan, man, how long has it been? Almost since high school, huh?"

The two embraced. Jonathan was with two other guys whom Joseph recognized, but whose names he couldn't recall.

"Joe, come on, man, you know you got to come and chill with us for a minute. We're just headin' into the bar for a couple drinks."

Joseph thought about it for a moment as the waitress walked up behind him to hand over his leftovers. He had actually been looking forward to getting back home, but he also knew that there was nothing awaiting him there but dark clouds and misery. The idea of just hanging out with old friends, and maybe holding his troubles at bay for a few more hours, sounded pretty nice.

"Yeah, let's do it. I've been wondering where you been all these years, man."

The foursome entered the bar and began ordering drinks. Joseph immediately realized he had not had any hard liquor in nearly five years. He quickly thought to himself, "Should I just order a glass of wine? I don't want them to start laughing like I'm a softie, though." When the bartender came to Joseph, who was luckily sitting on the end, he just spat out what Jonathan, who was sitting next to him, ordered: "Long Island for me, too."

The fellas sat and reminisced about old times. Classes and teachers that they liked and disliked, but most of all, girls.

Jonathan was the most vocal. "Man, Joe! Have you seen Shalice lately? That girl is fine now! I know she used be all chasing you around the campus back in the day. I don't know what she saw in your skinny ass, but if you saw her now you would be like, DAMN! She ain't all bony no more like she was back then. She got it goin' on now!"

"For real? Man, I haven't seen her since graduation. My sister saw her at the mall a couple years ago. She said she had changed a lot. So what you been up to, Blackwell? You married, or what?"

"Na, man, I ain't hardly got time for no wife. I'm out here trying to make this paper. I've been gettin' busy in the studio, you know, producing some groups."

"You ain't got no kids yet?"

"Yeah, man, I got two. One of them is in Florida though. I might go out there this summer and see her. You know, try and handle my business. This other one is with Nicole."

"Crazy Nicole Cooper? You still kickin' it with her? Man, I forgot all about you two. Y'all still together?"

"Now, I didn't say we was still together. You know, we just be kickin' it sometimes. She was just trying to trap a brother getting pregnant, you know. I had to let her know, I ain't the one for all that."

"Well, why are you—" Then Joseph stopped his sentence. He had questions about his friend's situation, but the possibility of coming off preachy was heavy on Joseph's mind. After all, they certainly had no idea that their old friend was now an ordained minister. And for some reason that suited Joseph just fine.

"Why what?"

"Nothing man, don't trip."

As the conversation continued, the drinks kept coming, and

before he knew it Joseph was on his fourth drink. The guys had all moved from the barstools to the dartboard, and whoever came in last each game had to buy the next round of drinks.

Joseph had now moved from tipsy to flat-out drunk, and it showed in his dart throwing. Three throws in a row he completely missed the board. What followed each throw was a roar of trash talk and laughter that could be heard throughout the bar and out into the restaurant. Joseph himself appeared to be just as amused at his intoxication as his three comrades. A number of times he nearly fell down in laughter at his own ineptitude. After dispensing with the sixth round of drinks, the foursome was informed that it was two o'clock and the bar was closing. Although he was heavily intoxicated, Joseph was aware enough to know that under no circumstances could he drive himself home.

Joseph questioned Jonathan as to how they were going to get themselves home, to which Jonathan replied, "The same way we always do, very slowly."

"What, are you gonna drive?"

"Yeah, I'm gonna drive. Shoot, I probably drive better drunk than I do sober. I sure do drive a lot slower. I already got one DUI. If I get another one they might send my ass to jail. But what the hell, you only live once, right, J? You want to ride with us? We can drop you off at the crib if you don't wanna drive your car."

Joseph was shocked at the simplicity of their solution, and even in his sorry condition he knew enough to pass on the poor proposition. But what struck him most profoundly was the statement that we only live once. Joseph knew in his heart that he had never been taught that, but it seemed undeniable that his last few hours of recreation had been based on just that premise.

"No, I'm cool. I think I'll just drink a cup of coffee and sober up a little," knowing full well it would take more than coffee to make him capable of driving.

After the fellas stumbled off into the street, Joseph was left with the real situation of how to get himself home. The restaurant was closing, and he knew he couldn't sit there much longer. Even if he was close enough, he couldn't walk home. He would surely be picked up by the police as he staggered. That would be a nice story for all the people whom he had preached to. The only idea he could come up with was to call James.

When James picked up the phone he was surprised at who was calling him at such an odd hour. "Joseph, where are you at this hour?"

"Man, I'm at Shari's. I need you to come and get me."

"Are you drunk?"

"Yeah, a little. I ran into some of my folks from high school and we was just chillin' in the bar, you know."

James didn't try much to mask his contempt in his short reply: "Don't go anywhere, I'll be right there." Joseph was still saying thank you, even though James had already hung up the phone.

As James drove to the restaurant he decided to call Joseph back on his cell phone and tell him to come outside so he wouldn't have to park. When he called the phone rang four times then went to voice mail. James called again but this time someone answered after the third ring.

"Hello?"

"Hello. Who is this?"

"Um, Just call me Bill? Who is this?"

"Okay *Bill*, This is James Quincy. Where is Joseph?"

"Joseph? Oh, you must mean this drunk brother sitting here leaning up against the wall."

"Why are you answering his phone? Put Joseph on the phone!"

"Well, he don't look like he's in the condition to conversate right now. I think it would be best if he just slept for a while. He looks like he's had a little too much to drink this evening."

James quickly becoming agitated at the stranger raised his voice into his own cell phone as he drove.

"You don't need to worry about what's best for him! Why are you answering my friend's phone anyway?"

"I don't know? I heard a phone ringing and I answered it. It's a real nice phone too."

"Man, if you don't put my friend's phone back where you got it I swear I'm going to..."

"What? What are you going to do? Keep on shouting?"

"Brother I tell you if my mamma hadn't raised me right I would find you and bust your behind!"

"Well, lucky for me I guess. Speaking of mammas, I think I'm going to call my mamma right now. I haven't spoken to her in a while."

"You're going to call your mamma at 2:00 in the morning?"

"She's a night owl. She likes to watch Jerry Springer."

"I'm sure she can't wait to hear from her baby, Bill the cell phone thief!"

When James pulled up, Bill was long gone. Joseph was sitting outside the restaurant, leaning on a streetlight. When James helped him into the vehicle, Joseph immediately began to thank his friend and poorly tried to explain how his predicament had come about. James said nothing as he drove. When they pulled up in front of Joseph's house, he was still rambling about high school stories when James finally cut him off.

"Joseph, man, look. You can't be doing stuff like this. This ain't you."

"I know, Quin, I know. I got to handle my business."

"I know you're having trouble dealing with all this stuff going on right now. I know it's tough, but you got to be smart. You've got a lot on the line, and I don't want to see you throw it away. You're taking the low road, man, and sometimes when folks take the low road they get lost."

Joseph let out a big sigh and stared out the window. James continued, "Now you know you got to meet with that cop tomorrow afternoon. You got to make sure you talk to this guy so we can know what we're dealing with. You know he's doing this as a favor."

"Quin, you right, man. I really appreciate you helping me out and coming to pick me up like this and stuff. . . . Man, I got to...I got to throw up!" At that, Joseph jumped out of the car and ran toward the door, still stumbling and looking for his keys. He made it as far as the bushes, which served as the toilet. James could clearly hear each groan and whimper on the quiet street. As he drove off James watched in the rearview mirror as his friend checked his pockets with a bewildered look, likely searching for his cell phone.

Chapter 18

There was another group, seemingly off in a corner somewhere, who exposed the corruptions of power. They're the ones who were reviled, imprisoned, driven into the desert, and so on. It was only much later that the evaluation was reversed and they were recognized as the true prophets.
Noam Chomsky

They met at the police station just after two o'clock in the afternoon. Mr. Kelley was to begin his shift at three. Joseph and Mr. Kelley decided to take a walk around the block as they spoke. They wanted to ensure the confidentiality of what they were discussing. Before going into details about the recent events involving his son, Joseph wanted to make absolutely certain that their conversation was not on the record, and that, regardless of Mr. Kelley's outlook on what had happened, he would not make his knowledge public, or attempt to force Alfonzo to testify. The officer politely agreed. Mr. Kelley then informed Joseph that he had two young children of his own, and he couldn't imagine what he would do were he faced with a similar situation. At this, Joseph was convinced of the police officer's sincerity. He went into his story, not sparing any of the details. When he was finished, Mr. Kelley plainly showed genuine empathy for the young man he had never met, empathy reminiscent of James Quincy's reaction to the tale not so long ago.

After regaining his composure, Mike told Joseph what he believed to be the most important aspect of the event: "Exactly how well the young man saw the perpetrator is what's important. What exactly did Alfonzo say he saw of the guy?"

Joseph responded, "He said he saw his black vest and blue jeans and a tattoo on his right forearm. He also said that the guy had long braided hair and he was wearing a lot of jewelry." Mr. Kelley thought for a while, and then suggested to Joseph that, while it was not a bad description for a crime scene, with the exception of the tattoo, most of the things Alfonzo saw were aspects of his appearance that could be easily changed. If the perpetrator had any intention of evading arrest he had probably changed much of his appearance by now.

Mr. Kelley went on to tell Joseph that "the people working the case had a short list of individuals they suspected of being guilty, but with little to no evidence their case was going nowhere. Unfortunately, so many young people had tattoos nowadays that unless he got a really good look at it, it wouldn't be of much help. Did he say anything else that might narrow the field? A car he saw, or a scar?"

"No, there was nothing else."

"Did the guy say anything that could be incriminating?"

"No, he said that the guy just kept saying, 'Now what you gonna do, now what?'" They continued walking, and mentally going over their options, when Joseph realized he had left out some information that might be valuable.

"But the guy whom he was pointing the gun at said something, I completely forgot. Alfonzo said that Bobby Humphreys, as he pleaded with the guy, said, 'C'mon D, I wouldn't do that to you and da man.'"

"'C'mon, D, I wouldn't do that to you and da man?'" Mike brought his hand to his chin, somewhat confused over the newest information. "I've got a suspicion of just who 'D' could be, but 'you and da man?'"

"Yeah, he said the guy said it real funny, though, like, 'you and da meean.'"

Right away Michael Kelley's countenance was altered. He looked up into the sky and sighed heavily, as Joseph still wondered what to make of the strange statement.

"He wasn't saying 'da' meean.' He was saying 'Damian.' 'I wouldn't do that to you and Damian.'"

Joseph was astonished. "Damian! Oh, how do you know that?"

"Damian Bonds is a well-known hoodlum around this town. This young kid has got his hand into everything from drugs to stick-ups to I don't know what."

"You mean Damian Bonds, the athlete?"

"That's the one. A lot of people remember him from his high school sports days. The boy was All-State in two sports. Had his pick of over a dozen scholarships for either basketball or baseball. Do you remember his older brother De' Andre?"

"Vaguely. I remember my father telling me once that he had gone to see Damian play and his big brother was in the stands with his friends wreaking havoc on everybody around them. He said that they finally had to throw him out when he started picking fights."

"Well, as your son can attest, he's still wreaking havoc."

"No, is that the shooter?"

"That's our man, no doubt about it. He was actually a pretty solid athlete himself back in his day, but he was such a head case no coach wanted to deal with him."

Joseph just stood listening with a fixed look of fascination on his face, as Mike continued speaking.

"You know, I've really got to tell you. We've been looking to get this kid off the street for a long time, but I don't know if you want to mess with these two. What your son has got on De'Andre would be enough to do a lot of damage in a case, *a lot of damage*, but, man, these are some pretty tough customers we're talking about. They might not be afraid to hit back once they see who's hurting them."

By now the two had stopped walking and were standing facing each other. "I'm going to have to think about this. You understand? I just don't know."

"Hey, I understand. I don't know what I would do, and I'm a cop. Whatever you decide, man, is on you. Nobody's going to hear from me that this conversation ever took place. And just so you know, if you do decide to come forward, you can't let anybody know you talked to me before doing so. It wouldn't look so good to my superiors, you get my drift?" Joseph then assured Mike that their conversation would remain confidential, regardless of his decision.

That evening Joseph decided at long last to call his sister to inform her of what had transpired with her only nephew. Rather than call his grandparents and other loved ones, he opted simply to sit back and let the news travel through typical family chatter. Joseph purposely made his and Alfonzo's presence scarce for the night, so as to not have to answer any phone calls and explain how he didn't know for sure what his plans might be. Father and son decided to go out to dinner and take in a movie afterward. Throughout the night there was no mention of Bobby Humphreys, De'Andre Bonds, or anybody else who had to do with Friday night. The only thing Joseph had decided for sure was that there was no need to tell Alfonzo of what was currently being considered by his father until the decision was made. In the wake of such trying events, the two were able to appreciate one another's company much more than they ever had in the past.

The next day Joseph had a change of scenery for his young son. As soon as Alfonzo returned home from school, Joseph told him to go and change his clothes.

"We've got some work to do outside. I'm going to introduce you to manual labor."

Alfonzo replied in a tone that suggested obvious confusion. "Manual who?"

Joseph, in the midst of laughter, "Manual labor. Haven't you ever heard of him?"

"No. I had a friend named Manuel when I lived at my grandma's house. He was Mexican."

Joseph, continuing to laugh, responded, "Well, this manual ain't Mexican, and he sure ain't gonna be your friend."

The two went outside and started trimming, sweeping, pulling, and mowing. Although Alfonzo didn't appear to be enjoying the exercise very much, he didn't complain. Each time he felt he might be nearing the end of his task, Joseph informed him of the assignment he could begin next. After several hours of drudgery, the two laborers were surprised to see Allen Shaw, Sr. pulling up in front of the house. He strolled up and complimented Joseph and Al on their effort. Joseph politely informed their visitor that his son preferred to be called Alfonzo rather than Al, and Mr. Shaw obliged. After making some small talk with the workers, Mr. Shaw and his grandson decided to have a seat on the porch and talk. Meanwhile, Alfonzo, at his wit's end, expressed his discontent with manual, who had obviously opted not to show up and be of any assistance whatsoever.

Allen Shaw dug right into the thick of things.

"I heard what happened. How are you guys holding up?"

"He's holding up a lot better than I am. I think I'm going to be a wreck by the time this thing is all over."

Joseph then explained to his grandfather the conversation he had had with Police Officer Michael Kelley.

"I don't know what to do. I don't want to put him through any more, I really don't."

"You don't think he can handle it, or do you think his life might be in danger?"

They went back and forth with questions and answers, Joseph continuing his inclination to forget that the night ever took place. Allen, Sr. finally posed the question he knew his son wouldn't want to face. "Have you taken this question to God yet?"

Joseph sighed, then crossed his arms across his chest. "Look, I feel that what God would want me to do is to take care of my son. The last time I spoke to God, he didn't speak back, and that's okay, but I just need to take the easy road for a change. I mean, I feel like I've been looking down the barrel of one gun after the other and I'm tired of it. I just got to do what I can to get the devil out of my life and Alfonzo's life, once and for all."

"Joseph, I understand what you're going through, I do. But the truth of the matter is that you can flee the devil all you want, but if you're not running to the arms of the Almighty, then you're just running in circles." Mr. Shaw put his hand on Joseph's shoulder as he spoke softly to his grandson. "I'm not trying to tell you what you should do. I'm not trying to tell you what you should tell your son. I've been watching you drift farther and farther away from me and your grandmother, from the church, from God, from everybody who cares about you, ever since that woman showed up at your door. You need to know that there is no need for you to be ashamed of the way things have turned out. On the contrary, your grandmother and I respect you even more for stepping up and dealing with this thing the way a man should. You've been walking through a dark forest for a while now and there's no reason you need to be walking by yourself. You have a family that loves you."

"I know. I never felt you guys were ashamed of me. I just haven't been able to be around anybody much lately you know. I don't know if I've been angry, or afraid, or ashamed, or maybe all three. I think I just needed to be by myself for a while."

"Well, that's all right. We all feel like that sometimes. Just know that you're making decisions for both you and Alfonzo right now. You don't want to close him out. You guys have both managed to make the best out of the storms that have been blowing your way. You don't want to start caving in to doubt now. Not now. These are the times that God uses to help us grow. He helps us grow closer to himself. I know it's hard to see when you're standing in the middle of it, and there's pain and fear all around you so deep and thick that you can't see straight, but now is the time when you need to go to Him. Be still before Him and ask Him, what is it You would have me do."

"But what if he doesn't tell me?"

"C'mon, you know better that that. He'll tell you all right. You just have to make sure you're listening for *His* guidance and not to your own fears and worries. Let me tell you something. You have been in the church all your life, from when you were a baby. I'll bet you can count on your fingers the number of days you missed in church as a child. But when was it when you came to God?"

Joseph responded without hesitation.

"When I was on that road listening to the radio."

"That's right. It was when you were going through something that nobody could help you with but God. Joseph you have had a good life. You, me, our family have had some good times together. But it's not the good times that strengthen us. It's the hard times. All those Sundays you sat in church. All those sermons you heard. None of them made God as clear to you as when you were hurting and you needed God's comfort. And it's the same with people. When people go through tough times together, it changes the relationship. That's when you know you can count on somebody. You and Alfonzo are eleven years behind in your relationship but trying to shield him isn't going to help you get where you're trying to go. It may very well keep you from getting there."

He paused for a moment, allowing Joseph to contemplate his words. Then he continued. "What often looks like the hard road often turns out to be the road we were built to travel on."

Joseph half smiled, and replied to his grandfather. "My buddy James calls that the high road. He said that God tries to put us on the high road but we usually choose the low road."

"Yeah, well, that low road might look good, but trust me, I've had my tires popped on it many of times."

They laughed and embraced each other. They continued with some light-hearted conversation for a short while. Then, before leaving, Allen Shaw forced a promise out of his grandson to seriously consider the advice he had been given.

Chapter 19

A man who is good for anything ought not to calculate the chance of living or dying; he ought only consider whether in doing anything he is doing right or wrong
Socrates

When nightfall came, Joseph found himself hesitant. Alfonzo was already fast asleep. Joseph sat quietly in the living room. He tried to read, but found it difficult to concentrate. He repeatedly noticed the time on the grandfather clock that had been in the same corner of the living room for as long as he could remember. As the pendulum swung near and far, Joseph made every attempt to honor the wishes of his grandfather who cared so deeply for him. The more he examined himself, the more anxiety pressed in on him. His heart scoured his barren soul, touching all the corners of his consciousness, but there was nothing. The desert was dry, and his spirit was withered.

He then retrieved the Bible from the bookshelf. It was his dad's Bible from years ago. Allen Shaw, Jr. had received it from his father when Granddad first became a minister. The inscription was still inside the front cover. "*Allen, this is your gift of life. The purpose of this book is to help you to get to know God. Only then will you recognize his sweet soft voice when it calls to you. Only then will you recognize him at work in your life. Love, your Dad.*"

While Joseph flipped through the pages of the book, he prayed, asking God to speak to him. He kept flipping quickly through the pages, too fast to see the words, then he stopped. He opened his eyes and began to read. "Then we will no longer be like children, forever changing our minds about what we believe because someone has told us something different or because someone has cleverly lied to us and made the lie sound like the truth. Instead, we will hold to the truth in love, becoming more and more in every way like Christ." He paused, pondering the words. Hold to the truth in love.

"Is this God speaking? Is this what I need to do, hold to the truth?" The words were clearly relevant, but the fear was still overwhelming.

Now down on his knees, Joseph voiced his quiet anger. "How can I ask my son to do this? How can I risk his life for this truth? I'm just getting to know him. He's just getting to know me. And I'm supposed to ask him to put his life in jeopardy for truth?" Joseph then caught himself, and realized his tone of voice. He stopped and rubbed his hands over the Bible covers. What had been a confrontation, turned to pleading. "Lord, I'm begging. Let me bear the brunt of this burden. Don't allow my son to be held accountable for my fears and weaknesses."

Joseph got to his feet and headed to his bedroom, ready to end his lonesome trek through the wasteland, but something forbade him to go. He was stuck. He could not leave things as they were. Instead of going to his own bedroom, he went to Alfonzo's room. There he brought the boy to awareness, then whispered to him, "I have to go out for a moment; I'll be back shortly." Alfonzo simply nodded and fell back to sleep. Once in his car, Joseph had in mind only one place to go. He headed to De Angeles Memorial Church, where he had spent a considerable amount of his life since childhood. He hadn't been there in several months. Except for the time he had spent at college, this was surely the longest span in his life he had gone without making an appearance in the beautiful tabernacle. The time was only eight o'clock, and he had some concern about the church members he might run into. He wasn't in the mood to hear "Haven't seen you around here for a while; where have you been?" or "How is fatherhood treating you?" but still he did not turn around. He knew that it was where he needed to go. When he arrived at the temple there were a few cars in the parking lot, but not many. As he walked up the church steps he saw and greeted a few members whom he recognized, but the conversations were kept brief. He could hear children's voices coming from the main floor of the sanctuary, so he opted to take the stairs to the balcony. As he had hoped, it was empty.

Right away, Joseph realized that down below, the children's choir was in the middle of rehearsal, and it was none other than his grandmother, Crystal Shaw, directing the way. He watched for a moment as the children tested her patience at every opportunity. Of the many services he had witnessed inside that church, it had been over fifteen years since he had seen one from the balcony. He thought back to when he would sit up there with his friends as a young boy and write notes back and forth, sometimes to girls, sometimes to his buddies. He walked the length of the upper floor, taking in the barrage of memories, listening to the children struggle to maintain the pitch that their instructor had demonstrated to them. Joseph finally sat down in the last seat and put his head in his hands. He once more returned to that barren wasteland to retrieve the precious thing he had voluntarily forfeited not so long ago. As he sat, Mrs. Shaw, who was being turned in every direction by unruly kids, caught a glimpse of her adored grandson sitting alone. She was fully aware of the dire circumstances that had befallen Joseph and his son and she felt immediate empathy. As she watched him sitting still in the darkness above, her heart went to him, and, standing in the middle of chaos, she said a prayer.

When she had finished, Mrs. Shaw demanded order in the room. She went out into the hall and called in some of the children who had shown enough mastery of the song to deserve a short break. Mrs. Shaw then told the children that she wished them to practice a rendition of their opening song for the upcoming musical. As she spoke, Joseph's head remained in his hands, oblivious that his grandmother had witnessed his presence. The children whined and complained that they had practiced the song more than enough, but she insisted it needed to be done again, "with feeling!" As the pianist queued up the song, a young girl not yet a teenager, wearing a simple pair of blue jeans and a loose white blouse, walked to the front of the platform.

Somehow Joseph didn't recognize the sweet music being played on the piano. Each chord soared majestically into the air and throughout the tabernacle, but he could not grasp them mentally or spiritually. It wasn't until the child began to sing that he recognized the song.

I will lift up mine eyes to the hills
From whence cometh my help
My help cometh from the Lord
The Lord which made Heaven and Earth
He said He would not suffer they foot
Thy foot to be moved
The Lord which keepeth thee
He will not slumber nor sleep

Her divine voice flowed deeply into the desert where Joseph's spirit had been held captive, and enraptured it. He looked down on her in complete solemnity.

Oh the Lord is thy keeper
The Lord is thy shade
Upon thy right hand,
Upon thy right hand
No the sun shall not smite thee by day
Nor the moon by night
He shall preserve thy soul
Even forever more

At this instant the complete choir joined in the chorus with the young girl. Although they supplied more force than melody, it was her lead that continued to make certain that the rhapsody was fit for an audience of the most heavenly of angels.

My help
My help
My help
All of my help cometh from the Lord.

Joseph closed his eyes, and although his countenance remained solemn, inside he leaped for joy. He knew his stint in the desert had come to its close. As he listened to the sweet messengers graciously deliver his divine epistle, he began making his way down the stairs and onto the main floor. He walked directly up to Mrs. Crystal Shaw and greeted her with an embrace that she knew was born of renewed love.

Finally, Joseph's estranged love had not *returned* because He had never left, but He made His presence known by shouting his name from the heavens so clearly and beautifully that it could not be mistaken. Where before there was darkness, now he saw light, the color of hope. From that present awareness until he was fast asleep in his bed, Joseph was reengaged in a tender doxology more delightful than most would comprehend.

The next day Joseph made sure he was home before Alfonzo. How would the boy react to what he was about to be asked to do? When Alfonzo walked up the steep flight of stairs that led to his home he knew that something was brewing. His dad was standing in the doorway, not reading the paper, not reading a book, just standing. He was relieved to find out, first of all, that he was not in trouble. Joseph had gone over many times just the correct words to use to explain to Alfonzo the responsibility that was required of him, even if his friend Shannon was unwilling to bear the same cross.

"Two young men are dead, son, and if we don't take a stand and tell what you saw, nobody is going to pay for what happened." When he finally understood what it was that Joseph would have him do, Alfonzo agreed with less distress than Joseph would ever have expected. Alfonzo explained that he had been haunted nightly with thoughts of the gruesome experience.

"Maybe if I do something to help put that guy in jail or something, I won't have to always be thinking about him. Maybe I could start thinking about how I helped get that guy for what he did."

Joseph was well pleased with his son's outlook on the situation, but he was convinced that the boy had a limited idea of the danger involved with taking the stand he was planning to take. Without making too much of the risk, Joseph tried to give his son an idea of exactly what he might be in for.

"These guys aren't going to take lightly to you going into court and telling people what their friend did, and even worse, other people might even say that we're both crazy to even go up against these guys, but I'm going to tell you a little secret. I know everything is going to turn out all right. God stands by people who trust in him when things get tough like this, and he's going to stand by us."

Joseph couldn't help the little twinge of guilt that hovered about him. He still didn't believe that his innocent young son had any realistic clue of what he was in for.

Chapter 20

Let's eat pomegranates until our hands turn red, and all we can think about is getting the juice off.
Mozelle Batiste (Eve's Bayou)

The police station was crammed with people hustling about taking care of tedious errands that most persons would never care to know about. When Joseph and Alfonzo finally located the detective office that was in charge of the case they found two men who appeared more interested in paperwork than police work, in the child's opinion. They sat at their computers only vaguely looking up to acknowledge the presence of this man and son who had walked in. After waiting a few moments for what seemed like nothing to be done, one of the officers finally asked, "So what can I do ya for?"

Joseph feebly spoke up. "Well, my son here saw something Friday evening that we think you might be interested in hearing."

The other officer who had previously not taken any notice of his visitors suddenly became interested. "Is that right? You got something you'd like to share with us, son?"

Alfonzo stood silently. It wasn't until Joseph assured him that things were fine that he spoke up. "Yes, sir. I saw a man get shot."

The surprising words clearly took both officers off guard. The one sitting farthest away got out of his seat and walked over closer to sit

ROD LOCHÉ

on the desk right next to Alfonzo. The other more senior officer looked directly at Joseph as if to ask "Are you sure you want to do this?"

Joseph maintained his sincere posture. He knew that he and his son were doing what needed to be done and there was no more room for doubt.

The story that followed astonished the two policemen. They had already given up hope of anybody coming forward with information regarding the murders of Bobby Humphreys and Greg May. Now they knew they would have a real opportunity to send a murderer to prison.

The meeting lasted for over an hour. Every detail of the infamous night was gone over two, three, or four times. By the end of the meeting both detectives were impressed with the amount of information retrieved, and even more impressed with the willingness of this father and son to come forward. They assured absolute anonymity for the boy until his day in court. Joseph was also promised that any assistance he felt the least bit necessary would be instantly granted. Joseph requested that information concerning the case be communicated back and forth via his friend on the force, Michael Kelley. The detectives both agreed. The slight fear Alfonzo had brought with him into the meeting was nearly completely gone by the end. What replaced it was excitement that arose upon seeing the immense importance being placed on every word that fell from his lips. The two were now entrenched in the battlefield, and there would be no turning back, regardless of the size or strength of the opposition.

Joseph and his family, to keep their thoughts away from the trial, filled the next few weeks with numerous mundane activities. They went away for a week to visit family who lived hours away. They went bowling, ice-skating, whatever came to mind. Alfonzo was becoming accustomed to answering plenty of questions each day when he came home from school. Any suspicious occurrences were to be immediately reported to the authorities.

Alfonzo had a difficult time at school making small talk with

162

Shannon. He attempted whenever possible not to be left alone with his one-time best friend because Alfonzo knew that whenever they were alone Shannon would want to discuss the events of that chilly Friday night. Alfonzo had been told that it would be a bad idea to tell Shannon that he had gone to the police. To have word get out would be a significant mistake, and by Alfonzo's own opinion, Shannon was not to be trusted. It was over Joseph's disapproval that young Alfonzo was attending school at all. It took overwhelming coercion to convince Joseph that keeping Alfonzo out of school altogether would bring about too much suspicion.

On the second day back to school, Shannon told Alfonzo about how a policeman had come to his home and questioned him about where he was on Friday night. "The cops just asked me about what I was doing Friday night and I told them I just went to the arcade and my bike got stolen. They asked me if you and I did anything else that night, and I said nope. Then they said if they came across my bike they would call me."

Joseph was sure that his friend would put together the fact that he had already spoken to the police, but Shannon never figured it out. The fact that Shannon had no clue as to what had taken place led Alfonzo to believe that his street-smart friend might not be quite as sharp as he had once thought. But Shannon was still prone to offer his advice.

"Look, Alfonzo man, if the cops ever show up at your house asking about that night, just tell them we went to the arcade, my bike got stolen, and we walked home. That's it and we're in the clear, man."

Alfonzo just nodded in agreement. He felt bad having to lie to his friend, but he had been assured by more than enough people that he was doing the right thing and that it was Shannon who was the coward.

Michael Kelley was surprised, but happy; to hear that Joseph and his son had come forward with their information. He made it clear that he would be honored to act as the go-between for the Shaw family. With each phone call, and each meeting, he informed Joseph that they were doing everything possible to speed up the process and get the trial underway. De'Andre was now behind bars, and luckily, he too was pressing to get the trial started as soon as possible. After three weeks had gone by, Alfonzo was finally asked to meet with a district attorney. They would go over his statement and let him know what to expect in the courtroom. Joseph and Jasmine sat in the meeting with Alfonzo to lend their moral support. The next day the Shaw family was informed that the court date had been set.

On the day of the trial, Joseph couldn't find his keys. He thought he knew where he'd left them, but they were not there. With his tense voice, he enlisted Alfonzo to assist in the search. Five minutes, ten minutes, twenty minutes spent looking, Joseph was beginning to lose his cool.

"They were right here! I know it! Are you sure you didn't move them?"

Alfonzo just shook his head and quietly whispered, "No, I didn't touch them." After frantically emptying three kitchen drawers, two that had little if any chance of containing the heavily-sought-after keys, Alfonzo finally approached his father and reminded him, "Dad, don't worry about the keys. Mr. Kelley will come and pick us up if we call him." Joseph looked at his son, and felt the freedom from fear and agony that children so readily offer to worrisome thinkers. He hugged his son and told him once again how proud he was of the stand that he was taking.

At the courthouse, Joseph was directed to leave his son in a heavily-secured room with the assistant district attorney and a broad-shouldered security officer. Joseph himself entered the courtroom along with Officer Kelley. They sat near the front. The gentlemen didn't talk much, but instead watched the various reporters and family members file through the door. Jasmine soon entered alongside Allen Shaw, Sr. and his wife. They took seats in the only area available, the back. At last, just before the trial was to begin, in walked Damian Bonds with a number of cronies beside him. Joseph knew who he was at first glance. He was tall, and dressed in expensive clothing. The young, handsome-looking man scanned the room as he coolly walked to his seat, as though he was looking for someone in particular. When he sat down, his older brother, who had just been led into the room in shackles, turned to happily acknowledge his presence.

Joseph listened as the family members of the two slain boys complained and objected to all the statements presented by the defense. De'Andre sat quietly, maintaining a calm look of disinterest. Joseph couldn't help wondering what types of thoughts were cycling through his mind. Is he sorry for what he did, but unwilling to show his conscience in front of his friends? Or is he genuinely an animal and just considers this the life he chose to lead? Either way, he was a murderer, and no tears would be shed when he paid the price for his actions.

It was two hours into the trial now, and Joseph began to wonder how Alfonzo was holding up, crammed into a room full of strangers. It was at least comforting to know that the Assistant DA was a woman who appeared to be well accustomed to keeping company with children. But finally, there was no need to worry any more. The prosecutor was calling his star witness.

Into a deadly silent room walked the twelve-year-old boy, ready to destroy modern society's dedication to impassiveness over justice. All eyes were focused on him. Damian Bonds watched with an expression of surprise. Whether it was surprise that the boy was so young, or surprise that he was even present, was not known. As he was sworn in, Alfonzo looked toward the ground. He made no eye contact with anybody. Joseph was mildly surprised that the boy even knew which hand was his right. The prosecutor began with questions regarding how the boys had ended up on that particular street the night of the incident.

"Alfonzo, where did you go on Friday night, October the 12th?"

"I went out to the arcade with my friend Shannon. I didn't have permission though."

"No, you didn't have permission, did you? So why did you go without your dad's permission?"

Alfonzo still felt badly about leaving the house that night. He continued to look down as he answered. "I don't know. My friend

Shannon said it would be fun, and that everybody from school would be there."

"Well, I'm sure your dad has forgiven you for that. We all make mistakes. Tell me how you got to the arcade."

"We rode Shannon's bike. I rode on the back, but it got stolen while we was there."

"It got stolen. So then what did you do?"

"We started walking home, but then some dudes pulled up that Shannon knew and they said they would give us a ride."

Alfonzo was asked to give a very in-depth description of the two young men who had pulled over to offer them a ride home, the goal apparently being to lend faces and personalities to the victims.

As he spoke, Alfonzo worked hard to look at nobody but the attorney. He thought that he would like to look around and acknowledge his dad and family members who were surely in attendance, but he didn't want to risk catching a glimpse of an angry De'Andre Bonds.

Finally, the time came to talk about the shootings. Again, Alfonzo was asked to be as detailed as possible. As he described the voice of the gunman standing in the center of the street, the boy's voice began to slowly crack, and then fade out. The attorney politely asked him to "take a breath," then to "speak a bit louder, please." Alfonzo described the hairstyle that, surprisingly, the defendant was still wearing. He then gave a vague description of the tattoo on his arm and the clothing he wore. But these were not the most damaging words. What was to come next would be. When asked what Bobby Humphreys said as he pleaded for his life, Alfonzo repeated just as he had heard it:

"Look D, c'mon, man, you know I wouldn't do you and Damian like that."

At this, both De' Andre and his younger brother closed their eyes and mentally conceded that their ordeal had worsened. Murmurs spread throughout the room. For the first time Alfonzo gazed into the audience and caught a glimpse of his father. He also caught a glimpse of De' Andre. The young man had his head down in his hands. For a brief second Alfonzo felt sorry for the person he appeared to have brought so much grief to, but before the sympathy could catch hold, in the blink of an eye it seemed, the defense attorney was there directly in front of his face.

"Is that all you heard Bobby Humphreys say that night?"

Alfonzo was caught off guard. "Huh?"

"You said you heard him say 'Look, D, C'mon, man, you know I wouldn't do you and Damian like that.' Is that all he said?"

Alfonzo paused to consider the question. "No, he said some other stuff too, but—"

"Like what?"

"Well, he was going on so fast I couldn't tell what else he was saying."

"But you're sure he said, 'Look, D, C'mon, man, you know I wouldn't do that to you and Damian?'"

"Well, at first I thought he said 'I wouldn't do that to you and da meean,' but…"

"Oh, but they told you he was saying 'Damian,' didn't they?"

"Well, they asked me if he could've been saying 'Damian.'"

"What about your friend Shannon? Where is he?"

"He said he wasn't going to tell nobody. I think he was scared."

The examination kept on at a steady pace, with the DA objecting here and there whenever possible. When the testimony was over, and the man who had been asking so many questions at a ferocious pace finally went back to his desk and took a seat, Alfonzo looked over toward his father and smiled. Joseph fought back tears of gratitude and appreciation as his son was excused from the stand. While Alfonzo was being escorted from the courtroom, he saw out of the corner of his eye that a man was staring at him. The man watched him all the way to the exit doors. His eyes were hard, and his brow was lowered. Being the object of such pure hatred was a feeling Alfonzo would not soon forget.

Moments later the Shaw family gathered into Alfonzo's secured room. Hugs, kisses, and pats on the back were lavished on the upholder of justice. Alfonzo reveled in his accomplishment. They opted not to stay for the rest of the trial, and left the courthouse under heavy security.

That night, Joseph and his son slept at the home of Allen and Crystal Shaw. Jasmine made a special visit over to the house specifically to take her brave nephew out for ice cream. The two invited Joseph, but he declined, allowing them to enjoy one another's company alone. As they sat near the window waiting for the delivery of his strawberry sundae and her root beer float, Alfonzo talked freely about the day, how nervous he had been, and how glad he was that it was all over.

While he spoke, Jasmine found herself watching two young men standing outside having a smoke. One wore a baseball cap facing backwards, and the other had his hair in braids. She felt a nervousness come over her. As she intermittently nodded to her nephew, she considered what the two young men were doing outside the ice cream shop and whether there were any police nearby. The two men slowly started walking toward where Alfonzo and Jasmine were seated. As she watched the men, Alfonzo continued talking and dipping into his sundae. They walked up close, right outside the glass. Jasmine took in a deep breath and looked around the shop to see if any help was nearby. The two men kept walking, and as she cautiously turned to look over her shoulder she saw them hop into a vehicle and pull away. It was then that she realized they had never even appeared to pay her or Alfonzo any attention whatsoever. She felt foolish.

When she turned her attention back to her nephew he seemed to be in deep thought. "So, what you thinkin' about?" The reply she received was much more than she had bargained for.

"Why do you think my mom is never around?"

Taken aback by the gravity of the question, Jasmine sat up straight in her chair. "Wow, I really can't say for sure. You know, I've never actually met your mom." Alfonzo's expression became dejected. Jasmine then responded to his sorrow. "You know, some people have trouble finding happiness. I mean, I'm sure your mom loves you, but maybe she can't find what she thinks will make her happy."

"Well, can't she be happy with me?"

"Yeah, when I say she can't find what she needs I don't mean she's not happy with you, I mean that she wants to add to what you two have. It's like her heart is finicky. First it wants this and then it wants that. When she finds something that will make you both happy it only lasts for a little while, and then she wants to find something else. My father used to call them butterfly hearts, fluttering from one thing to another. Never settling on one thing for very long."

"Well, do they ever find what will make them happy?"

"Uh, yes and no. You see, the trick is not to find out what will make you happy, but how to be happy. You see, there is nothing out there that is gonna make you happy for very long. What you have to do is learn to be happy no matter what your situation. Do you know what I mean?"

"I don't know, but I think so."

"It's like, tell me something you wish you had that would be really cool."

"That's easy. Playstation 2."

"Ah, a Playstation 2. Your cousins are always hassling me about that thing. Well, what I'm saying is that if you were to actually get a Playstation 2 you would be happy for a while, but sooner or later there would be a Playstation 3 or a Super Playstation, or something like that. Or there would be something else to come along in your life to make that Playstation 2 not all that exciting any more, and when that happens the happiness that the Playstation 2 brought you will start to fade away. So what we have to do is learn to be happy whether we have the latest games or the latest clothes or the latest anything or not, and then nobody can take it away from us."

"Oh, I see what you're talking about. I had a friend back home that had an eighteen-speed bike. It was cool, and he never even rode it. I wish I had a bike like that. I guess he just got tired of it."

When the two returned home, everybody was still ablaze with talk about the day's events. Alfonzo managed to maintain his feelings of honor, but could not shake the eyes of hatred that had invaded his innocence as he was leaving the courtroom. He also grew uneasy after overhearing numerous bits of concern expressed to Joseph concerning their safety. Questions of security and safeguards were beginning to cause the youngster to wonder just what kind of danger it was that might be lurking behind every door. Michael Kelley promised the Shaw family he would ensure that the police kept on alert for any suspicious behavior in the neighborhood, and also on the activities of Damian Bonds.

Jasmine felt the need to talk to Joseph about the conversation she had with Alfonzo while out for ice cream.

"Joseph have you spoken to Alfonzo about his mom?"

"Of course! Give me some credit! Why would you ask me that?"

"Look, I'm not trying to question what you're doing or not doing. I just wanted you to know that he's still having a tough time with it, you know."

"Yeah, I know. The truth is she's gone. I don't know where to and I don't know when she's coming back. There's not a whole lot that I can say to him that's going to help. I don't know what else to say to him?"

"Have you tried at all to track her down?"

"Look, I tried to find her, but it's not happening. She moved away from the place she lived when I was in Texas a few days after I left. I don't know any of her friends. I don't know what to tell you. I don't know where she is!"

"Look I'm not trying to be in your business! I'm just trying to help! You don't have to get all pissed at me!"

Joseph knew that his anger was misplaced, but he chose not to respond. He just folded his arms and looked away.

Then an idea popped into Jasmine's head. "Hey, you said his grandmother raised him, didn't you?"

"Yeah he was pretty close to her."

"Well, where is she? Do you think we could find her?"

"I don't know? He said that she got sick and had to go into the hospital."

"Little brother, I think it would be worth your while to find out where she is! If he could talk to her, or maybe even see her, I'll bet that would do wonders for Alfonzo!"

"You know, you have a point. He would probably love to see her. But goodness, I don't know where to look? I mean, what should I do, just start calling every nursing home and hospital in Texas?"

"I don't know, but we need to do something. Come by my house tomorrow. Your big sis will give you a hand."

Chapter 21

If I knew you and you knew me
And each of us could clearly see
Through the inner light divine
The meaning of your life and mine
I'm sure that we would differ less
And clasp our hands in friendliness
If I knew you and you knew me
Howard Thurman

Within days the trial was over, and De'Andre Bonds was found guilty of two counts of murder in the first degree. The end of the trial brought hope that the episode had finally come to a close. The man had been found guilty, and no act of violence could change it. The only reason for fear was the possibility of pure revenge.

At the church service on Sunday, Pastor Louis Wendell presented both Alfonzo and his father with plaques, and honored them before the whole congregation for their heroism and dedication to right conduct. The assembly roared with approval, and many of the members even shed tears upon hearing of the courtroom bravery of the boy. Joseph shared an embrace with Pastor Wendell that was long overdue. It was an embrace that said I love you far better than words ever could. The congratulations from members of the congregation continued for days. Well-wishers, hearing of the valor of both father and son, heaped blessings upon blessings on them both.

Regrettably, neither Joseph nor Alfonzo could fully embrace the good cheer that followed them, for both were preoccupied with nagging thoughts. Alfonzo was still contemplating the venom-filled glare he received as he exited the courtroom, and Joseph was wondering how much longer it would be until he could be at ease with the physical safety of his young son and himself.

It was on a Thursday evening, and Joseph and Alfonzo had gone to the library. They were searching for books for Alfonzo to use in his report on reptiles. The kids were allowed to choose their own topics, and although Joseph had made numerous enriching suggestions, his son was bent on discovering snakes. The outing had produced many fact-filled books. Alfonzo was sure he had all he needed to put together a worthwhile report. He bounced ideas off his dad as they parked the car and walked toward the house. Joseph then told Alfonzo he had an extra special surpise for him. Alfonzo's excitement was apparent in his voice.

"What is it? You got me a cell phone?"

"No, I didn't get you a cell phone. But I know you're going to like this surprise."

"You can't even give me a hint!"

"A hint, you want a hint?"

But upon nearing the porch Joseph realized that there were two men casually resting upon the steps.

Joseph froze. Alfonzo continued walking and talking, not noticing the strangers at hand. When he realized that his dad had stopped, Alfonzo took a second to find out what had stolen his dad's attention. When he saw the two men, who had now risen to their feet and were coming toward them, he was gripped with panic. It was him! The one who had, with a single glance, given him a clear perception of hate. His first impulse was to run, but they were now much too close. Alfonzo could only back up toward his dad, steadily keeping an eye on the approaching men.

Joseph scanned the area and realized, like Alfonzo, that running was not an option. There was a vehicle parked nearby, with two more young men standing outside. No would-be eyewitnesses could be seen anywhere, and the sun had already begun to set. Joseph felt his heart quickening as he clutched Alfonzo nearer to him.

Damian Bonds slowly walked up to them. He appeared nonchalant. He took slow drags from his cigarette as he stared into absolute fear. His associate wore a cap pulled down low, so that his eyes could barely be seen. His arms, covered with tattoos, were big and tense. More noticeable than all the rest were the handguns shoved into both men's belts. The guns were shining, and placed so that they could be easily seen.

"So what's up, Rev? You know who I am?"

Damian's voice was unusually low and raspy for such a thin man. Joseph paused, looking around. His first impulse was to not answer, but he didn't want to enrage the man in front of his son.

"You're Damian Bonds. De' Andres' brother."

"I guess my rep travels." The relaxed youngster laughed a little as he took another drag from the cigarette and blew smoke through his nostrils. "You had to be expecting a visit from the family of the recently imprisoned, I'm sure. You know how we gangstas is. We hate to let an eyewitness get away. Even if I am a little late."

Joseph made his decision. He had better make an attempt to get Alfonzo away from them right now. He couldn't wait another second.

"Look, Mr. Bonds. My son here was only doing what I told him to do. Please let him go into the house and I can stay here with you guys."

"Nah, I don't think so, Rev. I want to deal with you, and I want to deal with him. You know, I didn't believe the little man was gonna have the guts to go up there, but he did, didn't he?" nodding to his buddy. "He went up there and told everything. I was like, damn! This little fool ain't no punk!" Damian paused again for another puff of smoke. He then shifted his eyes toward Alfonzo as he continued to talk.

"You know, the lawyer said my brother was probably gonna get twenty-five to life. That is, if he can escape the death penalty. He said they don't usually give niggas the death penalty for shooting other niggas. Now if he would have shot a white boy, his ass would be in that chair right now! Ain't that some shit! You know what else he said? He said that there was no way they would have been able to even bring him in for questioning if it hadn't been for little Alfonzo here."

Joseph again spoke up. "Look, he didn't even know what he was doing. He's just an innocent child who did what his father told him to do. Please don't take this out on him."

"He didn't know, huh? But *you* did, didn't you? You knew what you was doing when you told him to go up there and say what he saw, didn't you!" Damian's voice began to rise. "You religious folk, always putting your nose where it don't belong, Rev." Damian began pacing around the yard. As he spoke, his aggression was clearly rising.

"You know, my mama used to go to that church y'all got. She used to praise your granddaddy. Oh, Reverend Shaw this and Reverend Shaw that! She would put her hard-earned money into that collection plate every Sunday and we wouldn't be eating nothing but bread and fucking Spam out the can on Monday! I couldn't stand that shit! They should have been giving *us* money, not us giving it to them. I never could understand that. After that she got sick, and she would be going to the doctor it seemed like every day to me, right? I still remember my aunt telling me that she was going to be with God soon, any day now. But every day when I went to see her she was still there, talking to me, laughing, and asking me how school was that day. My aunt told me later on that it was your granddaddy who was coming to that hospital damn near every day to pray with her. She said the doctors didn't know what was keeping her alive. She stayed alive long enough to see my diploma when I graduated from elementary school. She was so happy, I thought she was gonna get up and dance. She probably didn't think I would get that far."

Joseph calmly interjected: "Prayer is a powerful thing."

"Well, if it's so powerful, why did she have to die at all, huh? Why did I have to go and live my life with some punk-ass father I never even knew before? Why is my brother sitting in a cell waiting to find out if he's gonna live or die?"

"Well, son, God has his ways."

"I don't want to hear that! How does that help me? That's

bullshit!" Damian had now yanked the gun from his belt and gripped it tightly. He gestured dramatically with his gun in one hand and the other hand tightly clenched into a fist. "You see this gun here? This is my God. People bow down to it, they give me money because of it, they worship it. This is all I need. This is how I make sure the bills get paid. You feel me, Rev? And my bills stay paid!"

Damian threw his cigarette to the ground and rubbed it out with his foot. He then motioned to Alfonzo. "Come here, little man." When Alfonzo started to move slowly toward Damian, Joseph held him back. Damian pointed the gun directly at Joseph. "I told him to come here. Be smart, and don't piss me off." Joseph released his grip and Alfonzo timidly walked over toward the gun-bearing Damian. Damian then knelt down to speak to the boy face-to-face.

"Was you scared when you was sitting up there in that courtroom with all them people watching you?"

"No."

"You scared now?"

"A little bit."

"You know, most people wouldn't have done what you did. They would have hid under their bed and acted like they didn't see nothing, like little bitches! Did your daddy tell you to do what you did?"

Alfonzo looked back at his dad. Joseph nodded his head to his son "yes."

"Yeah."

"You know, your daddy is a brave man. I don't think he's too smart, but he is a brave man." Damian stood back up to face Joseph. He then told his friend to wait for him with the others. The big tattooed man first objected, but then conceded when Damian repeated his order again, louder than before.

He continued speaking to Joseph, but with his attention focused elsewhere; he appeared to be speaking more to himself. "You know, Rev, I really wasn't sure what I wanted to do with you two even on the way over here. My brother Dre', he was out of control. Them two fools he shot—it wasn't really over drugs or over money. It was really because he just didn't like neither one of 'em. He was a hard brother to handle. Even when we was kids he was hard to handle, but after he got into snortin' he just got even worse. The truth is, things might be better for him and me both with him on the inside. Hell, he ain't gonna have to worry about nothing in the joint. Three hots and a cot, that's all he needs." Finally Damian returned his stare and his attention to Joseph. His voice was sinking into a somber monologue. "You, Rev, I could take you out like I started to, but what for? You just ended up doing something that's probably better off for both me and Dre'. Besides, if I smoked you, then this little crumb-snatcher here would probably end up in some fucked-up home situation just like I did. I guess what I'm saying is, I'll see you around."

Just as suddenly as he had appeared, Damian Bonds departed. As he walked off, Joseph hugged his son tightly. Alfonzo's eyes had begun to water, although he hadn't made a sound. As Joseph clung to his son he heard Damian call to him from across the yard.

"Say, Rev, as long as you seem to owe me one, why don't you make it a point to mention a brother next time you conversatin' with the man upstairs?" Joseph smiled, and assured the young man, "I'll do that for you, absolutely!"

Joseph smiled again as he held his son close, and gazed up into a thousand flickering reminders of the power of God, and he was thankful.

Chapter 22

I understood how a man who has nothing left in this world still may know bliss, be it only for a brief moment, in the contemplation of his beloved.
Viktor E. Frankl

The next weeks were an endless chain of moments, each one more precious than the last. An imposing burden had been shed, and both father and son found it a little simpler to locate the silver linings. Alfonzo and Shannon had less and less contact with one another until their relationship finally ceased altogether. Joseph soon found his spirit to be in such an altered state that he mourned for his oblivious past. He had dedicated years of his life to being a servant. He had done his best to model his life according to the principles put forth by Jesus, but now he realized the limits of his faith. Now he realized that throughout all his preaching, and studying, and praying, he had never been a believer. He had never handed over the controls and enjoyed the magnificent gifts of perfect joy that one must experience to truly know and love the living God. As his head attempted to walk the skyward path leading toward Heaven, his heart had been firmly planted on the ground, tenacious and stubborn. Now the path was clear. The connection of compassion to the cerebral illuminated a way that led to a newer and better and truer salvation. God had shown himself in a way only possible when all the uncertainties of human existence were put aside.

Now it was time for re-dedication. It was time for Joseph to once again mount his horse and head in the direction laid before him by the Holy Spirit, just as a prior unbeliever had done on a dusty road to Damascus not quite two-thousand years ago.

Although he could not serve in his previous capacity at the church, Joseph was still an ordained minister. Because of nothing more than self-pity and shame he had turned down numerous invitations to minister and serve. No more would this be the case. Joseph knew he had a gift to touch the hearts of men with his words, and no longer would that gift be left to rot away in the cell of his remorse. Once again he began to study. The scriptures came alive more than they ever had in the past. Each passage took on new meaning. His friends and family all warmed themselves in the glow that radiated from his replenished spirit.

Enjoying a solitary lunch, and mentally making plans for the rest of the day, Joseph sat in his kitchen on a Saturday afternoon. Alfonzo had spent a customary morning with his cousins, and was due back any moment. Joseph couldn't decide if he was up for the movies or if he would rather spend the afternoon watching television or reading a book. His day was free until six o'clock, when James and a few other buddies would be over to study with him.

When the doorbell rang, Joseph was surprised his son had reached home so quickly. He had just spoken to him on the phone ten minutes ago. As he walked to the door he began to yell, "What, did you guys take a rocket ship to get here?" But as he opened the door he realized that his words were misdirected. Standing in the doorway was Sharonda. Quietness sat between the two for a number of seconds. Then, an awkward "hello" was forced out by the woman. Joseph just sighed and walked back to his seat, leaving the door open. As Sharonda gingerly walked in, she kept her eyes roaming from one side to the other, purposely not making eye contact with Joseph.

"Look, I'm sorry. I know you must think I'm a terrible person, but I had to get some things straight, and I knew you wouldn't want to be stuck like that. This was the only way I could do it. I didn't mean to put you in a bad spot like that."

As he responded to her, Joseph did his best to speak calmly, and not let his anger get the best of him.

"You know, you did put me in a bad spot, but it's not even about what you did to *me*. I can deal with whatever is going on in my life, but what about what you did to Alfonzo? That's just unforgivable. That boy was looking for you every morning, every night, and every second in between. You dropped him off with some man he doesn't even know. I mean, even though I'm his father, he still didn't know me. He was heartbroken."

"Well, I spoke to him that night before I left. I made sure he knew I was coming back."

"Yeah, but when? Did you tell him when you were coming back? He deserves more than that, a whole hell of a lot more."

"Look, Joseph, I don't need you to tell me what he deserves. It's not like this is the first time I've been gone for a little while. He knows I come back, and he knows how much I love him. You don't know what kind of relationship we have."

Joseph still maintained his calm tone, even though Sharonda had begun to tense hers.

"Well, as a matter a fact, he did fill me in on just what type of relationship you two have. He told me that he lived with his grandmother his whole life until she got sick and had to go into a home. Then you brought him out here."

"I don't have to explain how or where he was raised to you. Just because he lived with his grandmother doesn't mean I didn't raise him. I saw him all the time. What am I telling you for anyway?"

"You are telling me because I'm his father and I deserve to know!"

"Whatever! How about this? I'm going in there to pack his stuff and take him out of your house, so you won't be bothered with him any more. He's coming with me and Nate to L.A."

"L.A.? What's in L.A.? And who is Nate?"

"If you must know, Nate is my boyfriend and his cousin is in L.A. We're gonna stay with his cousin and his cousin's girlfriend until we get our own place."

"How long have you even known this Nate? Was he with you

180

when you dropped your child off on my doorstep?"

"No, he wasn't. I met him last month, and he said we could stay with his cousin in their apartment as long as we need to."

As Sharonda tried to walk toward the bedroom Joseph stepped in front of her. "Well, I have a suggestion for you. Before you go and start packing up our son's stuff, why don't you go into that back bedroom first and see what else you seem to have forgotten about."

Sharonda looked at Joseph and rolled her eyes before responding. "What is this, a tour of the house? Fine let me see what *else* it is I forgot!"

Sharonda stomped down the hall to the back bedroom. When she opened the door the shock that ran through her body briefly immobilized her. Lying in the bed was her mother. When her mom turned and saw Sharonda her eyes danced with excitement and she smiled in a way that Sharonda hadn't seen for years. Sharonda ran to her mom and hugged her tightly.

"Mom, what are you doing here? How did you get here? I'm sorry! I didn't know what to do?"

Her mom gently stroked Sharonda's hair as she hugged her and spoke in a soothing voice. "Hush child. It's going to be alright. I've been missing you too. Me and Alfonzo have been getting along just fine for these last few days."

"But that doctor. He said that you weren't going to make it. He said…"

"It doesn't matter what he said. I have a doctor in Heaven that overruled Dr. Taylor. That doctor said my time has not quite come yet."

"I love you, Momma! I'm sorry I wasn't there. I was scared!"

"I know, baby. We all get scared sometimes. But you have a child that needs you to be strong."

Sharonda stopped hugging her mom. She sat on the bed looking at the wall. She then questioned her mom. "Have you talked to Joseph about everything yet?"

"Well, I have spoken to him about some things, but I felt the most important things were best left between you and him. Do you understand what I'm saying?"

Sharonda took in a deep breath. Her mom continued talking. "That man in the next room is a fine young man. He's a man of God. He found out where I was and brought Alfonzo to Texas to see me. Once they got there we realized I didn't have any reason to stay there. I guess he thought it would be nice to have me around for Alfonzo's sake. The man in there loves Alfonzo to death, and I think he still has a place in his heart for you. He deserves the truth. Whatever you do from this moment forward, let it be with no secrets. Let it be with no lies."

Sharonda smiled at her mom. "You look real nice, a lot better than when you were lying in that hospital bed. I'm glad you're here and you're doing better, and I know Alfonzo is glad."

The two shared another hug and a sincere kiss on the cheek. Sharonda then got up and walked out of the room. She found Joseph sitting on the couch and she spoke to him. "I don't know how you did it, but thank you. Thank you for bringing her here, but she can't stay."

"I don't see why not."

"Joseph, there are things going on here that I don't think any of us are ready to deal with. We need to leave, all three of us."

Joseph took in a deep breath of frustration. He had hoped that the presence of Sharonda's mom would cause her to see things differently. "Sharonda, he's my son! We have a relationship! You can't just say, okay, playtime is over now, we'll be seeing you."

"I was hoping I wouldn't have to do this, but I'm sorry. The truth is that Alfonzo isn't your son." She dug in her purse and retrieved a piece of paper. "Here is his birth certificate."

Joseph put his hands to the top of his head, neglecting to take the paper from her hand.

"What! You've got to be joking! What kind of game are you playing here? He's not my son?"

"I'm sorry. I didn't mean for everything to turn out like this. I was just in a bind, and I didn't know which way to turn."

Now, for the first time, Joseph's voice began to rumble. "If I'm not the father, then who is?"

Sharonda then quietly sat down on the couch. She didn't answer. Her silence was all the answer he needed.

"Oh God, please, no! You mean to tell me you brought the son of the man who murdered my father to my home and had me look after him like he was my own son?"

Sharonda had no response. Joseph just stood still with his eyes closed and his body clenched tightly. His anger had mounted to such a bright red crescendo that it scared him. He struggled not to react to her in a physical fashion. He began searching himself. He searched for peace, and for wisdom, but above all else he searched for God's words to speak to him. In as calm a tone as he could manage he asked Sharonda. "Does he know?"

"Excuse me?"

"Alfonzo, does he know I'm not his father?"

Sharonda, getting a little attitude back into her voice, responded, "No, he doesn't know. He thinks you're the one. Shoot, I got better stuff to do with my time than to be driving him four hours back and forth every weekend to the penitentiary to see that no-good half-ass daddy of his. He ain't never getting out of jail, so what would be the point?"

Joseph continued with the questions. "How did you know my blood type? When you brought him here you said his blood type was A-positive, the same as mine. How did you know what my blood type was?"

Sharonda, in the most shame-faced voice she could muster, answered, "A friend of mine works in the administration office at the college where you used to go. She found it on some of your admission papers."

Joseph just stood silently fighting back the anger. Fighting back the tears. Fighting back the rage.

Sharonda got up off the couch and headed into the back room. Joseph glanced out the window, where he could see Alfonzo's makeshift dad-to-be leaning on a late model Honda Accord, smoking a cigarette. There were so many daydreams that had crowded Joseph's mind over the last six months about the future he and his son would share. There were so many memories they had created in that same six months. How could this be happening? He thought about the night Sharonda and the boy had first shown up at his door, and what a cold, rough exterior Alfonzo had. It had been months before the boy had let down his guard. But when it did finally come down, what a fine young man there was underneath!

What type of future was awaiting Alfonzo in L.A.? Living with strangers, probably sleeping on the couch or maybe even a cold floor. What were these people like? She didn't even know. With his face buried in his hands, Joseph began listening once again. Listening for guidance. Questioning everything he had once held to be sacred. "Every time I start to think I know what I'm supposed to be doing something else comes and turns everything around. I know I was lost, but I thought I had been found. I thought I was doing your will. Now what? When is this gonna end?"

Sharonda was in the other room gathering her son's few belongings. Belongings that he didn't have the day he showed up at Joseph's home. Joseph stood quietly trying to focus, and grasping for hope, but succeeding at neither. After about thirty seconds, he opened his eyes. The first thing he saw was the mantle over the fireplace. There rested their two plaques. The plaques they received from the church for standing up in the face of despair. Joseph thought about that day, and how happy his son had been. Together they had journeyed through the valley of the shadow of death, and indeed the Lord was with them. Amidst the jumbled web of confusion in his mind, suddenly a razor-sharp thought was dropped into Joseph's consciousness. The consideration was so clear and precise that it felt peculiar and foreign to him. The day they received the plaques, they were father and son, regardless of what anybody said or did. They were tied together in a bond that could only be the bond of a father and a son. So why not today? Why could they not be what they both needed to be for one another? Alfonzo needed a dad, and Joseph had only now realized that he needed his son. Joseph walked over to the room where Sharonda was finishing packing up her son's belongings, and he calmly spoke to her.

"I'm sorry, you're not taking my son from me."

Sharonda quickly turned to face him. "Excuse me, did you hear anything I said a minute ago? He's not your son! Y'all ain't family!"

"I heard what *you* said. Did you hear what I said? He is my son and you ain't taking him."

"I'm sorry. I don't know what it is you're trying to pull, but I hate to tell you, there ain't nothing you can do about it! He's leaving with me!"

"Sharonda, you might not know this but you've been gone for a little over six months. Do you know what that means? That means that Alfonzo is right now a legal resident of this county. That means that when I call child protective services on you, and oh, I'm gonna call, he has to stay in this county while they investigate the case."

As he spoke, Joseph's voice began once again to rise. "I want you to know that I am going to let them know every little tiny intimate detail I can strain my brain to remember about how inept you've been in taking care of this boy. About all the boyfriends you let play daddy and discipline him, about how you go for months at a time without seeing him, about how you dropped him off on my doorstep and disappeared in the middle of the damn night! And oh, yeah, you know what they'll do then? The first thing they're gonna do is drug test you. You see, I got friends in these places, I know how they work. How is that gonna go, huh? How you gonna feel about getting drug tested?"

Sharonda was shocked. "Why are you trying to do this to me? I said I'm sorry for leaving him for so long!"

"Yeah, but what about the next time? Who you gonna leave him with the next time, huh?"

"Fine, you think you can do a better job of taking care of him? Fine! You just give it a try! But don't come looking for me when you get tired of him and you don't want to play daddy no more, you hear me? Don't come looking for me!"

Sharonda threw the clothing and other belongings onto the floor and stormed toward the front door. She stopped short, then sat down on the couch and slapped her hands against her tear-stained cheeks.

Joseph just stood watching. The longer he watched the more he remembered how close he and Sharonda once were. The more he considered the disappointment on Alfonzo's face the day his mom walked out.

She then stood up and stared Joseph in the eyes. "Tell him I said I love him and I'll see him soon." With that, she continued toward the door. Through all of the resentment, he still felt sorry for her. Joseph wanted her to be around for her son. He also knew that there were still dormant feelings he held for Sharonda. Feelings he tried hard to ignore, but couldn't. She was his first true love. He knew he had to say something.

"Sharonda, why don't you stay a while? Let's see how it goes. Who is this dude Nate, anyway? I'm not saying we need to be together, I'm just saying we can work something out. For Alfonzo's sake we can come up with something better than this."

"Joseph, we both know that what I have to offer him right now ain't what he needs. I've got to get some stuff straight in my head first. I've got to make some changes."

"Going to Los Angeles with this clown you have waiting outside ain't going to give you what you're looking for. Come on, we can do this! The boy needs both of us. Let's at least take some time to talk about it!"

Sharonda then began walking toward the door once again. Suddenly the words phenomenally began pouring out of Joseph's mouth. They were words that to him symbolized the bond that the two had always shared. They were words that symbolized what was at stake this very moment. He spoke them calmly but forcefully.

"*I once felt I had found the bottom, the darkest night one could surmise.*"

Sharonda paused in mid-step. Rather than turning around she stared at the door in front of her. She listened for the next line. After taking notice of her reaction Joseph continued.

"*But I had not yet endured the fate Of premature goodbyes.*"

She turned toward Joseph and watched him intently as he kept speaking.

*"At God's request may Satan test the anchor of fragile lives. Heartfelt
petitions for my Lord's sweet mercy, but no hint of Heaven sent replies"*
Before he could continue Sharonda spoke up.

*"The victim of violent attacks was I the object of slander and lies.
Neither at its worst could instill the pain of premature goodbyes"*

They stood face-to-face, staring into one another's eyes.
Sharonda spoke softly. "Now, I guess we both have that poem
tattooed on our brains."

Joseph wanted her to stay. Regardless of the lies and the deceit, he
wanted her to stay. Through all of the pain and anguish Sharonda had
inflicted on her son, Alfonzo's love for her was unceasing. Because of
that, Joseph was sure that the relationship could be salvaged, if only
she could learn to really allow someone to love her. He was willing to
chance it, if only she could be willing as well.

Sharonda then spoke up. "The only problem is once you get as
accustomed to premature goodbyes as I have, they become a lot easier
to stomach. Take good care of my son—of our son. Let him know I
love him. Tell my mom I said I'm sorry. Goodbye."

As she headed to the car, Nate walked over to find out what was
keeping her. Suddenly, from the doorstep, Joseph could see Alfonzo
coming up the walkway alongside Jasmine. Nate had begun glaring in
Joseph's direction, but before he could take a step, Sharonda had
noticed Alfonzo, and instantly her demeanor changed.

"Hey, how are you doing, sweetie?"

The look of surprise on the young man's face spoke volumes.
Somewhere deep down he had never expected to see his mom again.
Now she was standing right there in front of him, as though no time
had passed since the last time they had been together.

Alfonzo loosely hugged his mom, still feeling more shock than
happiness. Jasmine stood back and, guessing who the woman was,
watched the interaction with a deep sense of curiosity. When the boy
didn't speak, Sharonda repeated her question. "So, how are things
going? How have things been?"

"They're going good."

Her nervousness was causing her to talk at a rapid pace. "Oh, I want you to meet Nate. Nate, this is Alfonzo, Alfonzo, this is Nate."

As the two exchanged handshakes, Alfonzo informed his mother: "Mom, I kind of prefer to be called Al now."

Joseph, hearing the conversation, couldn't keep from smiling upon hearing the boy's comment.

Sharonda, surprised, opted to go along with the request. "Okay, Al. Well, I just wanted to come by and see you. Me and Nate are going to go to Los Angeles for a while, but your dad thought you might want to stay here for a little bit longer. You know, at least until you finish out the school year and stuff like that."

Alfonzo just nodded approvingly.

"Well, it was nice to see you, though. Give me a hug, and Mommy will see you in a few months, okay? When I come back I'm gonna bring you a really nice present. You know, they got all kinds of nice stuff out there in L.A."

Sharonda quickly wiped away her tears and rushed into the passenger seat. Nate reluctantly got into the car after fixing one more glare in Joseph's direction. Alfonzo walked up to his dad and watched, alongside he and Jasmine, as Sharonda and Nate sped off down the street. Jasmine gave Joseph an unapproving glare, displaying her contempt for the boy's mother. She made sure to conceal it from Alfonzo's view. She then went into the house, saying she needed to make a phone call. As Joseph stood on the porch with his hand around his son's shoulder he once again considered the future in store for both of them.

Alfonzo, still looking down the street although the car was completely out of view, unexpectedly asked, "Dad, is she ever coming back?"

Joseph was surprised by the skepticism, but worked hard not to show it. "You know, I really don't know. I honestly believe that only God knows the answer to that question."

Father and son then turned and went into their house to enjoy lunch together.

Printed in the United States
70050LV00002B/247-258